W9-BBG-694

MAKING GOOD LOVE TO A BAD BOY 2

BREANA MORGEN

Copyright © 2019 by Breana Morgen

All rights reserved.

No part of this book may be reproduced in any form or by any electronic or mechanical means, including information storage and retrieval systems, without written permission from the author, except for the use of brief quotations in a book review.

❀ Created with Vellum

AUTHOR'S NOTE

Thanks for taking this crazy ride with me! In part one, we were introduced to all the characters, and in part two, we're about to dig into them some more. Just a warning – you will find yourself mad at the characters, disgusted with them, and in love with and rooting for some of them. Yes, Dom and Davion do some crazy shit, but what bad boy doesn't? I hope you enjoy this second installment – in my personal opinion, it's better than the first. And for those wondering, yes, there is inspiration for Domino Black, and he is my boyfriend of almost seven years and the father of my daughters. That man is crazy! He loves hard, he doesn't tolerate disrespect, and he rides for his family and friends. So, if you're wondering where you can find your own personal Domino Black, check Brooklyn, New York. They breed them there! Well, I'll let you get to the story, now! I'm excited to hear your thoughts, so please don't hesitate to leave a review and/or hit me on social media. Enjoy, and as always, happy reading!

SOCIAL MEDIA HANDLES

Facebook: Breana Morgen
Facebook Groups: Breana Morgen's Book Spot and In Reverie
Publications
Instagram: @bee_emdoubleu

OTHER BOOKS BY BREANA MORGEN:

Chapter One

DOMINO BLACK

y phone was ringing off the fucking hook, but a nigga's dick was getting wetter than the ocean, so I didn't give a fuck. It could've been Jesus calling me and I wouldn't have answered that motherfucker. Getting head from my girl with this Fruit Roll-Up on my shit was feeling too good at the moment, and whoever the fuck it was would have to wait 'til I busted this nut.

After decorating Bai's throat with some of my special sauce, I grabbed the phone off my dresser and finally scanned the missed calls. They were all from the same number, which was one I didn't recognize. Since they'd called my motherfucking ass back to back over ten times, I knew it was either about something important, or one of these hoes playing on my damn phone. When the number called the eleventh time, I answered, and a recording from the Columbia Correctional

Facility came on, letting me know my dumb-ass youngest brother was in jail.

When Baby D finally got on the line, I went in on his stupid ass. He was fucking up way too much for a nigga who wanted to go to the NFL. I bet it had something to do with drugs – lil' stupid motherfucker probably got caught with ecstasy or weed. I told him not to be fucking with Weezy and that bullshit. It was bad enough they'd gotten Weezy's mother-in-law's house shot up, but now that Davion was in jail, I was gon' have to go to Weezy's fucking head. And Davion's.

"Punk motherfucker! I'm coming up there to get yo' ass, but you better believe I'm fuckin' you and Weezy up on sight!" I barked into the phone, damn near scaring the fuck out of Bailee, who was laying her head on me, giving me soft kisses on my shoulder.

Even that shit wasn't soothing, though. I was hot. I worked too fucking hard to get Davion where he was supposed to be, only for him to throw it all away over some fucking drugs.

"Man, it ain't even got shit to do with Weezy, bro. Just... just come get me out. Please." The lil' bitch ass nigga was crying and shit, which was crazy to me because he liked to appear so hard. Davion was like a fucking boiled egg – hard on the outside, soft as fuck on the inside. That's 'cuz my mom and pops babied that nigga. Especially my mom. She thought that lil' motherfucker could do no wrong; I hope she's in

Heaven mad as fuck right now, 'cuz on my life, Davion got dumber by the day.

"What is it, nigga? What the fuck did you do?"

He couldn't stop whimpering long enough to tell me, so I hung up in his face. As soon as I got off the phone, Bai was on my ass too. She wouldn't let a nigga breathe, and times like this, I preferred to be left alone. But, you couldn't say that type of shit without hurting a female's feelings, so I just let it ride. I wasn't in the mood for her bullshit, either.

I pulled up my basketball shorts and put my Nike slides on. Bailee got herself dressed too, even though I never asked her to come with me. I guess that's why she was my rider – I didn't have to ask her to move a fucking muscle, and she was there.

"Did he ever say what he was in for?" She pulled up her lil' baby-ass shorts, which I didn't approve of. Those bitches had her ass cheeks out, and I'd have to kill a nigga for staring.

I shook my head and laughed. "Nah, but he did say it wasn't for no bullshit with Weezy, so who the fuck knows, man. Let me go grab some cash. I'll be back."

"So, you're gonna use the same money he stole from you to get him out of jail?"

"Nah. It ain't the same money, Bailee. 'Cuz he's got that."

She rolled her eyes and smirked. "You know what I meant, baby. That's exactly why Davion isn't gonna learn his lesson. Ever. You're always there to bail him out. He reminds me so much of Tyler that it's pathetic."

"Don't compare my brother to your bum-ass ex. At the

end of the day, Bailee, D ain't got parents and shit to help him out like you do. All he got is me. Now don't get me wrong, I will fuck that nigga up to the point where he wishes he was never born, but I ain't ever turning my back on him. That's family. And in order to be my girl, you gotta respect that shit."

I guess she felt bad for what she said, 'cuz she walked toward me and grabbed me from behind, trying to be all mushy and shit. We ain't have time for that though. I had moves to make.

"I'm sorry, Dom. Maybe that was insensitive."

I turned around to kiss her and smack her on the ass. "It's alright, baby girl. You can make it up by doing more of that Fruit Roll-Up shit later."

She giggled and gave me a kiss on the cheeks with her soft ass, juicy ass lips. Swear to God, Baby D better be glad I loved his stupid ass, 'cuz I didn't miss out on pussy for nobody. And Bai's shit was drenching wet, so it was ready as fuck for me.

I left the room to grab five g's out my safe, since I didn't know exactly how much his bail would be. I must've pushed a hundred and ten miles per hour, 'cuz we got to the detention center in record time. I was almost afraid to walk in there and see what the stupid nigga had gotten himself into.

Since I was a well-known motherfucker in Columbia, when we walked in, the bitch at the front desk already knew we were there for Baby D. I paid three stacks, and Bailee and I waited about two hours for that nigga to get discharged. The whole time we sat in the cold ass lobby waiting for Davion, my fucking phone was going off in my pocket, but I wasn't in the mood to check it. Whoever it was, was doing the most and annoying the fuck out of me, and what I didn't have was the energy to deal with it. It was probably nobody but that dumb-ass bitch, Tierra, anyway.

As soon as my brother came through the double doors to where we were, I smacked the fuck out of the back of his head.

"What the fuck, Domino? What'd you do that for, nigga?"

"What the fuck did you do to get in here, pussy?" I fired back, so hot that Bailee had to calm me down by rubbing my back like she did earlier. I swear to God, my girl's touch was the only thing saving this lil' nigga's life.

"I ain't do shit man. Let's go."

When we walked out the door, paparazzi greeted us with mics, cameras, and lights flashing in our faces. "Davion! How did you find yourself in the middle of a statutory rape case? Is your coach's daughter really pregnant? Are you ready to be a father? Did you know she was fourteen?"

Every news reporter in Columbia was there and in our faces, and I was taking in every question they were asking. If I found out this lil' clown ass nigga got a fourteen-year-old bitch pregnant, I was gon' kill his ass. I knew the lil' nigga was irresponsible as fuck, but damn; fucking around with a minor was unacceptable and quite honestly, nasty as fuck. No young bitch on this earth had a piece of pussy I wanted. Yeah, Davion had some fucking explaining to do. And fast.

Chapter Two

DAVION "BABY D" BLACK

As soon I got in the car with Domino and his bitch, he started talking all that bullshit, asking me questions that I wasn't in the mood to answer. Shit, I needed a minute to process all this shit myself, so I couldn't provide none of the answers to his questions even if I wanted to. I was so fucked up over the events that had taken place within the last few hours, and the only thing this motherfucker wanted to do was be on my case like he was my damn daddy. Dom still hadn't gotten it through his greasy ass head that no nigga, my blood or not, was gon' control me. And no nigga was damn sure not going to question me.

He kept asking me how the fuck I'd ended up fucking with a fourteen-year-old, and the truth was, I didn't know. Everything about this is fucked up, because Shanay told me she was sixteen, and she had the fucking body to prove it.

With ass and titties round and thick, the bitch had a body better than most of the hoes older than me. Then for the reporter to say she's pregnant...that shit had me shook. Shanay just saw me at the gas station and didn't say shit about a baby. She'd better be lying, or I was going to knock that fucking baby out of her. Wasn't no way in hell that a nigga was gon' have two fucking kids at eighteen. Hell, I didn't want the one Camiyah was claiming I had with her, but I knew if the lil' bitch proved I was her baby's father, I was gon' have to man up eventually. That wasn't gon' be anytime soon, though. I needed time to get over that shit too. I was still pissed off that Camiyah had managed to trap a nigga. I knew I should've strapped up with her hoe ass.

"Get the fuck out my car, motherfucker," Domino said to me, as he pulled up at the crib. I was glad he had enough sense not to take me back to my dorm after all that drama. I just needed to chill by myself and figure shit out before I went back to jail for murder.

Domino pulled off before I even had a chance to close the door behind me. I don't even get why that nigga was mad. It wasn't him who was at risk of having the words "sex offender" associated with his name for life. It wasn't him that had a baby by a trick and possibly another on the way by a fucking fourteen-year-old. It wasn't him who might get kicked off the football team, since all this shit happened with the coach's daughter. Shit, if I lost my spot on the team, I'd lose my scholarship. I wasn't the smartest motherfucker, so it wasn't like my scholarship was based on my GPA. But anyway, Dom was taking this shit too seriously 'cuz it wasn't him that was affected. It was me.

But fuck him. I had other shit to worry about. Like why the hell Camiyah's car was pulling up in the driveway right now.

"Camiyah. Fuck you doing here? Take yo' ass back home." I was liable to slap her ass back to the projects if she got out of pocket, so she might have wanted to take heed.

But, she didn't. Her stupid ass got out the car wearing a tight ass dress, like she was coming from the club. Shit, she probably was. Given the fact her baby was in NICU at the hospital, she shouldn't have been. But, hoes will be hoes.

When Camiyah walked up to the porch, she stood on her tiptoes and tried to kiss me, but I dodged that shit, making her stumble over her own feet. I'm quite sure she knew I didn't give a fuck, though.

"Well, hello to you too, Baby D. I tried to be a good baby mama and come check on you, since you're all over the news and shit for getting locked up, but I see you're on your bull- shit. I don't know why you treat me like this."

"You should be more worried about being a good mom and being at that hospital with your fucking baby." Her last statement wasn't even worth addressing. She knew why I treated her like this. I didn't respect hoes.

Tugging on her skin tight dress, she smirked and bit her lip, sizing me up. Camiyah thought she was slick, man. I could tell by the dress she wearing that she'd come over in hopes of giving me some pussy, but nobody wanted that damn Bloody

Mary between her legs. I clearly heard the nurse tell her six weeks, and that damn baby was nowhere near six weeks old.

"*Our* fucking baby." She pushed me like she wanted to get buck with a nigga or something, and although my pops raised us not to hit women, she was gon' get her shit rocked, fucking with me.

"Yeah, well, I need a blood test to prove it."

"You've been at the hospital almost every fucking day, Davion! You haven't accepted her yet? You are a father! *Her* father!"

I laughed and shook my head. "Nah. I'm a motherfucker who might have fertilized a seed. I can stand in the driveway every day, but that doesn't make me a car, does it? Fuck out of here with your bullshit Camiyah, alright? I don't need this tonight. Not from you or any other motherfucker. If you want some attention, go find a nigga on the street and get on your knees like yo' hoe ass mama."

"Fuck you! At least I've got a mama!"

Wham!

I knocked that hoe in the mouth for disrespecting me. I knew I was gon' have to hit the bitch, and that's why I wished she would've gone home like I told her to. But fuck it. She wanted my attention, now she had it. She had me fucked up if she thought I was gon' allow her to speak on my dead mom. Blood spewed from her lips, but I was unfazed. She should've watched her fucking words.

"Get the fuck away from my crib, Camiyah. Now!"

Since she wanted to be a crybaby and shit, I unlocked the

front door and slammed it in her face, leaving her crying on the porch. She shouldn't have crossed the fucking line, and maybe I wouldn't have had to go upside her big-ass head. Just as I was about to roll up a blunt, an eerie feeling came over me. I wasn't halfway done rolling before I heard some fucking commotion outside.

Pop! Pop! Pop!

I heard a car speed off after shooting at my crib, and suddenly I felt a lil' bad about leaving Camiyah outside. Not bad for her, but bad for me, 'cuz if she'd gotten shot and it turned out that I was her daughter's father, I'd be left to raise the lil' motherfucker by myself. Couldn't have that.

I quickly grabbed my strap and ran outside, but whoever the fuck had shot at the house was already gone. Camiyah was bent over on the porch bleeding from not only her mouth where I'd punched her, but now her leg too.

"Fuck!" I yelled, as I picked her up and brought her in the house.

I dialed up the ambulance and as we waited, I tried to wrap gauze around her wound. She was bleeding heavily though, but since I was just a leg injury, I knew she'd be alright. It was no doubt in my mind that Mike was behind this shit. I don't know how much more money that motherfucker wants from me and Weezy, but this was his second time shooting a house up trying to get us. With the way everything was going for me at the moment, I knew I needed to find a way to pay his ass before shit got worse. A nigga just couldn't catch a fucking break!

. . .

*T*he next day...

I was feinding for some coke, a blunt, maybe a pill...something to calm my nerves, but these crackers in front of me had me trapped in Camiyah's hospital room. Not to mention a nigga was clean out, and with the way I'd spending money lately, I needed to hit up Domino's stash again so I could refill my uh...medicine.

"So you're telling me you have no idea who would be shooting at your house, Mr. Black? Surely you've got to know something. Maybe...someone retaliating about your ongoing case with Shanay? You know, the fourteen-year-old you possibly impregnated." The bald, white motherfucker standing in front of me thought he was slick, throwing that bullshit in there. He knew just as well as I did that what went down at my house wasn't over no damn bitch. I just wasn't about to give him what he wanted. I was ready to choke that motherfucker – that badge didn't mean much to me. The only thing stopping me from hauling off and beating his ass was the fact that he had his strap on him, and I didn't have mine. "Answer me, Mr. Black. Do you have any idea who would be shooting at your home?"

"If I did, they'd be dead already," I lied. "Please excuse yourself, nigga; nobody's in the mood for the pigs' bullshit right now, alright?"

The cop smirked and nodded his head. "I'll leave. But I *will* be back."

I knew he knew I was lying, but I wasn't no fucking snitch. Yeah, Mike and his boys had been getting me and Weezy pretty damn good, but I was plotting on their asses, and I didn't need no fingers pointed in my direction when their bodies were found.

Camiyah grabbed my hand and lifted it up to her lips to kiss it. "Thank you for being here with me, Davion. It means a lot. Nobody wants to be in this situation alone."

She wasn't gon' be alone regardless, 'cuz all these doctors, nurses and cops wouldn't leave room 211 alone.

"You might not wanna be, but you're gonna be." I stood up and pulled up my pants, then dug for my car keys. "I was just making sure you were straight and shit, but I'm rolling out." I'd been at this motherfucker since last night and I needed a shower, to brush my teeth, and something to smoke on. If Camiyah thought I was pulling another all-nighter in this bitch with her, she had me fucked up. She wasn't my fucking girl.

"You're just going to leave me here, Baby D? Please don't go."

"Where's your family, man? Call them niggas. They care about you more than I do. I'm off duty." I tapped her on the leg, and she pushed me back down in my seat.

Here she goes with the dumb shit. This is exactly why I didn't want to be here with her begging ass anyway. You give a bitch an inch, they take five miles. These hoes can't never be satisfied with what you give 'em – they always want more. Number one reason why I don't try to please 'em.

Camiyah's sensitive ass started crying and shit, but I wasn't feeling it. "Shut the fuck up, man! Why you always crying and shit? Fuck is your problem, Camiyah?"

"I don't have family, Davion! You said it yourself – my mom's a hoe. Everybody and their daddy knows that. She'd rather be laid on her back than be here with me, or even taking care of me for that matter. And my sorry excuse for a daddy...I haven't heard from him since two years ago when he asked me for money for crack that I wouldn't give him. He told me to go to hell. So truly, Camia is my only family. And you."

And that was my cue to leave. I dropped my hand from out of hers and walked out before she could utter another word about me and her being family or whatever other stupid ass thoughts she had swimming in her head. Camiyah was just another hoe ass stripper in my eyes, and she'd never get the privilege of calling me her man.

Chapter Three

BAILEE RODGERS

I honestly thought things couldn't get any crazier than they had from last night when Domino and I went to get Davion out of jail, but I was currently being proven wrong. Domino had some business to take care of, so I was chilling at my parents' house for a while, and guess who had just rang the fucking doorbell, as if they knew I'd be here?

"Bitch. You've got some nerve coming to my parents' house. I suggest you leave before I give you the ass whooping of a lifetime." Those words sounded so good rolling off my tongue, but in reality, I was still in shock that I even had to say them to her.

Prior to my relationship with Domino, we'd never had any drama. Rhyan had always been someone I considered a best friend. Since meeting four years ago at freshman orientation at USC, I always had her back, and was under the impression that she had mine. I wiped her eyes every time they filled with tears over some fuck boy, and when she needed a shoulder to lean on, she had mine. Whenever she needed anything that I had access to, I gave it to her. But, I shared damn near anything except my man, and I felt like a fool for believing she understood that unwritten rule. I would've never disrespected her the way she did me, but I guess loyalty wasn't a two-way street.

Standing there wearing a stupid ass grin on her face, Rhyan was making the urge to kick her ass even stronger.

"What the hell are you doing here, Rhyan? I really want you to leave." I cracked my knuckles right in her face, so she could see I was getting ready to whip her ass. I had rings on too; the bitch really didn't want to fuck with me today.

"Bailee. I can explain." She folded her hands together like she was praying. While she was at it, she might want to ask God to spare her life if I got my hands on her.

I folded my arms across my chest as I looked at the bitch in disgust. I just couldn't believe I considered her a friend for so long. My anger wasn't even at the fact that she had a thing for Domino, because I mean, who in the city didn't? Domino was the type of nigga I called "universal fine", meaning despite your taste in men, Domino Black was fine to you. So, I knew going into this with him that bitches would crush on him. But my anger stemmed from the fact that my "friend" had gone so hard with her crush on my man, texting him from a fake ass Google number, and then coming by the club to see him. She was ready and willing to spread her legs that night, and had Domino offered, they would've fucked. That's the part that had me ready to whoop her ass. It's like she wanted him just because I had him, and she didn't care that I was getting hurt in the process. That wasn't a real friend.

I took a deep breath, so I didn't say anything I didn't mean. "Rhyan. I really want you away from me. There's no explaining at this point, alright? Fuck you. Have a nice life."

"Bailee. Your nigga came onto me. You can't be mad at me 'cuz these niggas are for everybody."

Wham!

Lying ass bitch. I hopped on top of Rhyan and started giving her a beating she'd never forget. I had her weave in one hand and was smacking the shit out of her with the other, watching blood seep through the corners of her lips.

My parents must've heard the commotion coming from the front porch, because my dad swooped me in his arms just as I was about to choke the living shit out of Rhyan. My mom went to Rhyan's aid, which is exactly what I expected her to do, being that my mom was someone who could find fault in everything I did.

"This isn't over, hoe!" I warned Rhyan as my dad carried me in the house. He sat me down on the couch and cracked a smile as he shook his head. He always did shit like that – he couldn't discipline me for my temper, because I was just like him.

Staring at my dad, I realized how he was becoming more handsome the older that he got. I was without a doubt a daddy's girl, and I was starting to see that I looked like him too. We had the same dark chocolate complexion, slanted eyes, and high cheekbones. My dimples were also inherited from my father. Now that he was starting to gray a little bit, he looked like an older Morris Chestnut.

"What the hell was that, Bail? I didn't even know you still fought. I haven't had to break one up since you were like fifteen." My dad chuckled and took a seat next to me on the couch, referring to the fight I got in with our old neighbors almost seven years ago. Before Rhyan, no bitches had tested me since they had, so they were the last ones to get that work. I still had it in me, though. And if Rhyan wanted part two, that could be arranged.

I laid my head on his shoulder as I let a lone tear fall down my cheek. Something about being cuddled up with my dad made me vulnerable. "It wasn't anything, daddy. Just a…a situation where I saw her true colors."

I hated not giving my dad all the full details, because before Domino entered my life, my dad was my best guy friend. I just didn't want to tell him everything behind the Rhyan incident because I didn't know how he'd feel about me dating Domino. All fathers wanted their little girls to be with someone caring, patient, strong, and who treated her like a lady. Domino Black possessed all those qualities, but he had a crazy, scary, rude side to him that I wasn't sure my parents would appreciate. Mainly, my mom.

"It was all over a boy! Really, Bailee? A boy?"

Speaking of the devil, she'd just stormed in, slamming the door behind her, speaking on something she knew nothing about. With one hand on her hip and the other wagging a finger at me, I felt like the child she thought I was.

I rolled my eyes and lifted my head from my dad's strong shoulder. I knew I'd better clear this up or else I'd never hear the end of it. "It wasn't over a boy, mom. It was over Rhyan's actions. She was disloyal to me, and then lied about it. Similar to what Aunt Lorraine did to you years ago."

Bingo. My mom wanted to act like she was holier than thou, but she must've forgotten that I knew my Aunt Lorraine, her younger sister, had a thing for my dad years ago. Her crush on him was so strong that she lied to my dad about my mom cheating on him, so he would leave her. What got her caught was that me, Tasmine, and two of our cousins were playing at our uncle's house and heard her on the phone plotting. Tasmine was old enough to know what was going on and after she explained it to my then thirteen-year-old self, I ran and told my dad. My mom and my aunt never spoke again after that, not even when my grandma passed.

My little comment must've struck a nerve with my mom, because she looked at me like she wanted to choke me, while speaking to my father. "You'd better talk to her before I do, Tim." She turned on her heel and walked up the stairs. When I heard a door slam, I knew for sure I'd pissed her off.

"What boy, Bailee? Not Tyler, I hope. That nigga ain't worth the time it took to throw a punch." My dad popped open a beer that was sitting on the living room table. "You want this one? I'll go get another."

I shook my head, declining his offer, but continued to

smile. My dad was the one who treated me like an adult. I turned twenty-one almost a year ago, and my mom still would forbid me to order an alcoholic beverage when we went out. She'd probably have a damn heart attack if she knew I was dating a strip club owner and was at his spot almost every night...

Since I didn't want the beer he offered, my dad took a huge gulp and then sat it back down. "Who is he? If he's a step up from Tyler, which isn't hard to be at all, I can deal with it. Talk to me."

I smiled, partly because I knew how much my dad hated Tyler, but held it in for my sake, and partly because just thinking about Domino always seemed to put me in a better mood. "He's really nice, daddy. He's a business man, too. And he wants to help me with making my dreams come true." My dad knew my dream was to do hair, so when I said that he raised his eyebrow and gave me a look that told me he wanted to know more, so I continued. "It's true, dad. He owns his own business. He wants to get me a shop and everything. I just have to find a way to break it to mom that I won't be going back to USC."

"Well you know how your mom is." My dad and I chuckled in unison. Personally, I didn't know how he'd stayed married to her for so long – she was so damn controlling. But, being that my dad was more laid back, I see how they balanced one another out. "Just make sure this is something you really want to do, Bailee. And if so, we'll be behind you one-hundred percent. But, don't leave it up to no nigga to make your dreams come true – you can do that shit on your own, too. I'm the only man you need." My dad gave me a kiss on the forehead and I breathed a sigh of relief, because if I at least had my dad backing me, that was enough for me. Between him and Domino, I had all the support in the world.

*L**ater that day...*
Since Domino had been having a rough few days, I decided to bring him lunch at The Black Palace, accompanied by a sexy massage by yours truly. I'd cooked a simple meal consisting of baked chicken, rice, vegetables, and cornbread muffins. He was going to be having me for dessert.

Wearing a tight, red tube dress that hugged my curves in all the right places, I applied my MAC Aaliyah red lipstick, spritzed some perfume on my wrists, and headed to The Black Palace with my cute picnic basket in tow.

When I arrived, there was a really pretty female with caramel brown skin and blonde streaks in her hair walking out. She was dressed like an undercover hoe. You know, one of those females who tried to look innocent, but would drop their panties for a nigga quicker than McDonald's dropped a basket of fries. I had no idea who she was, but given the fact that Domino's car was the only other one in the parking lot right now, I had questions. It meant they were alone, and I didn't trust hoes alone with my man, because they were always up to something. *Thanks, Rhyan.*

"Who the fuck was that, Dom?" I asked, barging in his office.

Domino looked from side to side and then behind me.

"Who are you looking for, Domino?"

"Whoever the fuck you think you talking to."

Asshole. I couldn't help but laugh, but I still needed my question answered. "Who was she, baby?"

"Bring yo' fine ass here. That bitch ain't nobody compared to you."

I never said she was, but I need her name...

He wrapped me in his strong arms, removing the basket from my left hand. Before I could utter another word, Domino's lips were pressed against mine in the most passionate kiss I've ever experienced. Feeling his tongue dip down my throat was erotic enough to make my vagina leak with juices. Had I been wearing panties, they would've been drenched by now.

Domino palmed my ass roughly and then laid me on the couch. Dipping his head under my dress, I felt his tongue saturating my insides. His lips against my lower set was making me throb from the inside with the way he hungrily sucked the juices out of me. When his tongue brushed against my clit, I felt a tingling sensation that was so robust it made my upper body go numb while my leg began to shake uncontrollably.

"Domino! Baby! Daddy! Yesss!" As I screamed his name he sped up his pace, and suddenly I felt my fluids leak from my pussy to his lips and beard.

Before I could regain my composure, he flipped me over

and began licking my ass with the same passion. As Domino told me one night when we were lying in bed – no area was off limits. Feeling his tongue dip in and out of my hole as he played with my pussy with his fingers had me crying tears of joy, because it felt so good. Never have I ever been stimulated like this.

I felt his large, meaty, dick enter me from behind, and for a moment I lost my breath. Ramming his pole inside of me roughly, yet slowly, Domino grabbed a handful of my wild, sweated out hair and pulled my head back so that I had a view of his sexy face. I loved it when he bit his lip as we fucked, because it showed me he was really into it.

"You know this my pussy right?" Domino pummeled me deeper and harder with each word he spoke. When I didn't immediately respond, he stuck all ten and a half inches of his thickness inside of me, causing me to belt out words and phrases I'd never ever said to a man. I think I promised *him* a wedding ring.

"It's…your…pussy…daddy." I finally got my words out as I backed it up on him and began to clap my ass cheeks together, while he stroked. "It's all yours."

Pulling my head harder, Domino licked my ear and whispered, "It better fucking be." I felt his cum fill my vagina, and when he let my hair go, I turned around to greet him with a kiss.

"It is, baby. I'm in love with you."

"I'm in love with you too, Bailee. Don't forget that shit, either."

Forget it? I was making a mental note of the date, time, and location. I damn near made my head hurt from trying to hold in my smile. I was trying not to show how excited I was that we'd said those words to each other, but hearing Domino tell me he was in love with me sent warm shivers down my spine. It felt different than when Tyler had said that shit to me during our relationship – this time when I heard it, it felt authentic. I could only hope and pray that he meant it, and that Domino Black would never become what everyone else presumed him to be.

Chapter Four

DOMINO BLACK

"You turning all soft on me, man. Next thing you know, Bailee's gon' be wearing your balls around her neck." Terrell laughed as he passed the blunt to me. The only shit I smoked was loud, and this fat ass blunt was filled with it, so I'd be high as hell in no time.

He'd better be glad I inhaled that motherfucker and calmed down a little, or I would've cussed his ass out. Terrell had been my boy since the days when we were thugging in our diapers, so he knew better than anyone that there wasn't a bitch on any of the however many continents it was that would ever run me. He was just fucking with me, 'cuz I'd told him Bailee told me she was in love with me earlier, and I slipped up and reciprocated. I'd never really been in love before, I don't think, unless you counted that shit with Sapphire. I think that was convenience and something to do out of boredom, more than anything. But this shit with Bail definitely felt different, and if it was love, cool; love wasn't gon' take my manhood away from me though.

"Shut yo' punk ass up, nigga, and finish loading so we can go."

We were about to leave his crib and go handle business, since that pussy nigga Mike was now doing some foul shit. Shooting up Weezy's lady's mom's house was one thing, but I was on that nigga's head for bringing his black ass to my parents' crib and doing that pussy-ass drive-by. Yeah, I wanted all the smoke. Tonight, Terrell and I were pulling up at his crib, and we didn't plan on having no mercy on that nigga. When all this shit was over, I planned to fuck up Davion and Weezy too, for bringing all this damn drama into my life. Clearly those niggas couldn't handle their mother-fucking affairs, and that was a problem for me. Davion's dumb ass was getting on my nerves. He was starting to always be in some stupid shit, and now his sloppy ass actions resulted in a shorty getting popped in the leg. Hopefully the lil' dumb nigga was by her side in the hospital, 'cuz I'm sure she got hit behind his bullshit. I didn't know who the broad was, because neither the news nor Davion released the name, but when I found out, I was planning to pay for her medical bills.

I finished loading my AK while Terrell finished loading his pistol. Shit like this used to give me a natural high back in the day. I've killed so many niggas, I could no longer keep count. Since becoming a businessman I've had to calm the fuck down a lot, but Mike and boys deserved what Terrell and I were about to give them.

My phone started ringing as we loaded Terrell's car, and the only reason I answered is because it was a number that looked familiar, but I couldn't place whose it was.

"This is Domino. Who's this?"

"It's me. Don't you have my number in your phone?"

"Bitch, what I have in my phone ain't none of your goddamn business unless you're paying Sprint every month. Who the fuck is this on my line and what the fuck do you want?" Some people would say I was too rude to people, but when shit like this was always coming through your phone, how could I be nice? Bitches loved playing on my phone 'cuz they thought it would make me want to play in their pussies, but that's not how a motherfucker like me operated. That shit got on my nerves and made me want to choke their dumb asses out.

"Domino! So you really don't love me? What about our engagement?"

Tierra. I was surprised she was calling me, because I didn't think she'd be leaving the mental hospital anytime soon. When I put her ass in there, I was banking on her being gone for so long she'd forget who the fuck I was. I don't know how they let her mental ass go. She wasn't playing with a full motherfucking deck.

"We don't have no fucking engagement, alright, T? I'd shoot myself in the head before I let you be the one to carry my last name."

"What about our baby?"

Click.

Baby my motherfucking ass. Tierra knew good and damn well she wasn't pregnant, and if she was, she'd better prepare to be a single fucking mother, or find the real father. I didn't let her fuck me without a condom, just so shit like this could be avoided.

"You ready?" I dumped the ashes from the blunt in the ash tray and tossed Terrell his keys. Flicked ass nigga couldn't even catch 'em. "Nigga you suck. No wonder you never got that basketball scholarship."

We could laugh about it now, since it was going on ten years later, but during our senior year, Terrell was dealing with this so-called recruiter for SC State, who promised him the starting position on the basketball team and a full ride, if he let him into some free concerts. At the time, Terrell was working part-time at The Colonial Life Arena, one of the most popular venues in the city. Terrell's stupid ass did it, only to find out the nigga he had no fucking pull at SC State, so he never got a scholarship. And he lost his job. Dummy.

"Fuck you, nigga." We laughed and headed to Mike's house, ready to send him and all his boys to their graves. The good thing about Mike's crib was that it was in the hood, so hearing all the gunshots we were planning to fire off wouldn't be a big deal to his neighbors and shit; therefore, no police would be called. Shit, if they called them, I doubt they'd even come. The pigs are scared of this nigga's neighborhood; that shit was *that* rough. I didn't give a fuck how rough his neighborhood was — I was about to light that bitch up like Christmas. Them niggas had fucked with the wrong ones.

When we pulled up, there were an ass of cars in the yard, but we didn't give a fuck. The more bodies we caught, the merrier. No mercy or no fucks were gon' be given; I didn't give a fuck if that nigga's wife and kids were in that bitch — everybody had to go.

Some motherfuckers liked to wear all black and hide their faces and shit, but not me. I knocked on that nigga's door wearing a smile as wide as his bitch's pussy with my gun in my hand.

"Oh shit!" Mike yelled, trying to close the door. But I had my size twelve Timberland in the way, so I kicked that motherfucker down.

"You wanna shoot shit up, homeboy? I came to join the party." I fired off rounds and so did Terrell, and within seconds, we had everybody in the house on the floor. Guts were splattered everywhere and so was blood, just like I wanted it.

That must've been those niggas' trap house or some shit, 'cuz there were drugs and money everywhere. I didn't give a fuck about those pills or that powder, but I did take some cash off the table. Peeling back a stack of over thirty one-hundred dollar bills, I dapped Terrell up as I broke him off half. That nigga had been warned not to fuck with us; I bet his dead ass learned his lesson now. I called my boys to come clean this shit up and get these bodies, and once they got there we dipped. Mission accomplished.

. . .

The next day...

I still had to get used to waking up with Bailee's ass in my bed. Well nah...her ass was fine. It was that big ass fucking hair that got in my way. That shit was always in my fucking mouth when I woke up. And when it wasn't in my mouth, it was right in my face when I opened my eyes. Some mornings I almost got my gun out, because I thought it was a possum in my damn bed. True, her shit smelled like fruits and vanilla, but a nigga wasn't trying to eat hair for breakfast every day. Sapphire used to wear one of those lil' bonnet shits, and although they were ugly as fuck, I needed Bailee to hop on that wave.

"Good morning, daddy." She rolled over and kissed me, getting a nigga's dick on swole. Morning wood was a motherfucker. Usually I didn't let those stank breath bitches come nowhere near my lips with their morning breath, but Bailee didn't have that issue. Shorty's breath was always minty fresh, and that was one reason I fucked with her.

After eating a quick breakfast, we showered together, then got dressed. I had shit to do, and even though laying up in that pussy sounded good as fuck, I knew I couldn't get shit done with her around. I had to finish up some shit at the club, then handle some other business that I didn't need her nosey, cute ass around for.

"Why can't I come with you to the club?" Bailee asked, after spraying her body with that vanilla scented shit she uses faithfully. Her lil' round, pretty face was scowled like she was mad or some shit, but that was comical to me. My bitch was already sexy, but when she was mad, she made me want to fuck her 'til she came all over my dick. I wanted to make her cream 'til she got glad in this bitch.

"You feel like sucking my dick?" I ignored her question. Pressing my manhood against her, I began to nibble on her ear. That was her weak spot.

"Nope." She pushed me back, trying to keep a straight face. I knew she wanted to laugh. No matter how hard she tried to fight it, Bai couldn't stay mad at me long. "I wanna go to the club with you, Domino. Why are you acting like you don't want me there?"

"Why you wanna bother me at work all of a sudden?" I knew the answer already. She was probably still tripping on ole' girl, Tatianna, from yesterday, but she had nothing to worry about. I fucked her years ago, and her pussy wasn't good at all. I mean on a scale from one to ten that shit was a negative five. She couldn't throw it back, she couldn't ride, nor did I feel her pussy lips wrap around my dick when I slid in her. So Bailee had nothing to worry about. Yeah, Tatianna tried me yesterday, but I told that hoe not to ever disrespect me by throwing that saggy pussy at me again. Yesterday, she was only at The Black Palace because I was in the process of interviewing people to manage my spot since I had to fire Sherita's ass. Tatianna might've been a loose pussy hoe, but her resume was as tight and right as one should have been.

I wasn't used to having to explain myself to nobody, so

Bailee's ass would just have to relax and let me work. Money wasn't gon' stop 'cuz my girl was feeling insecure.

"I'm not trying to bother you, Domino. It just seems like you're hiding something. I saw the girl coming out of your club yesterday, and you never told me who she was. You fucking her?"

"Nah."

That wasn't a lie. It wasn't the truth either, 'cuz I'd hit in the past. But, I wasn't fucking her going forward. Her pussy looked like an old person's face – I couldn't stick my dick in that again.

"Whatever." Bailee folded her arms and tried to walk away from me, but I tripped her ass up, making her fall on the floor.

Laughing at her ass, I helped her up, but she wasn't feeling me. "Come here, girl." I sat on the bed and sat her on my lap. "You know you're jealous as fuck, right?"

"How could I not be, Domino? Women practically throw themselves at you. Every. Single. Day."

"Who am I fucking, every...single...day?" I kissed her before she could answer, and began rubbing on her pussy. She had on a pair of those tight ass biker shorts I didn't approve of, so I stuck my hand in them and brushed across her opening. The pussy was hairless, just like I liked it.

"Stop...stop, Domino." Bailee tried to resist me, but if she thought I was letting that juicy pussy get away, she had another thing coming.

I picked her up and laid her on the bed. Gripping both

sides of her soft face, I pressed my lips against hers and she began rolling down her shorts. When all I was looking at was her perfect pussy, I kissed all over it before splashing her middle with my tongue. My tongue massaged her bud as I dived into her opening. Bailee was trying hard to resist me, but I had a good handle on her lower lips, so she couldn't get away.

"Uhhh, Dom. Baby, that feels so good." She swirled her hips in a circular motion and my face followed suit. I felt the muscles in her box clench, so I knew her release was underway.

Bailee palmed the back of my head with her soft hands and screamed my name as she creamed all over my tongue. I lapped up every bit. Her pussy tasted like nothing but fruit – Starbursts, actually. I could eat her box all day and never come up for air.

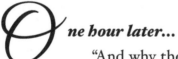

ne hour later...

"And why the fuck should I trust you to manage my spot? You can't even manage your pussy, 'cuz that shit looked run down when I hit it. Don't think I forgot."

"Because like you said yesterday, my resume speaks for itself. I've managed several spots, and could take yours to the next level. And as far as my pussy...you're funny, Domino. I was a little girl back then. I'm a grown ass woman, now. I manage my pussy just fine. I would offer to show you, but I like to keep it professional. *During interviews.*"

I was conducting Tatianna's second interview, and although I didn't trust that she managed her box, I did believe she could do the job of being the manager at The Black Palace with little to no effort. The experience on her resume ranged from management positions at restaurants and liquor stores, so a strip club shouldn't be too hard for her. After all, she used to work in one.

I met her when she was twenty-four, which would've been about five years ago. She used to come to The Gentleman's Corner when I first started working there. She was a bartender, then she quit to work at her family's business. While we were coworkers, we smashed one night in the parking lot, in her car. I was young. I was horny. But I know one thing − I was still horny when I left her ass. I couldn't even finish in the condom. I was mad as hell that night. Her pussy was on my "do not disturb" list; I wasn't hitting that ever again.

I nodded my head, satisfied with her answer, and began reviewing my notes. I'd held four interviews other than hers, but I couldn't doubt that she was the most qualified candidate. I just had to make sure she wasn't on no Sherita type bullshit, trying to mix business with pleasure, because if so, she was in for a rude awakening. "Do you wanna fuck me again, Tatianna?"

Laughing, she shook her head. "Absolutely not. I'm here to do business."

"That's what I wanted to hear. When can you start?"

"Today."

I reached across the table and gave her a handshake, closing the deal. I knew Bailee's jealous ass would have an issue when she came here and saw Tatianna as Sherita's replacement, but she'd just have to deal with it. Like I said, my money ain't gon' stop just because my girl is unhappy.

*L*ater that day...

I don't know why I felt compelled to buy Bailee shit when I knew I'd fucked up, but I did. I guess seeing her sexy smile made whatever I'd done seem trivial, 'cuz at the end of the day, I was making my girl happy. Not that I'd even done shit wrong, but just knowing she'd feel some type of way about Tatianna made me want to soften the blow. And the only way I knew how to do that was to buy a gift.

"That's the one I want, bruh." I pointed to a candy apple red, two-door Mercedes Benz Coupe that was parked at the front of the lot. That shit was smooth. I could see Bailee's cute, chocolate ass driving it. And that's exactly why I was about to buy that shit for her.

"You wanna test drive it first?" The car salesman asked, handing me the key.

"I don't think I asked to drive it. I told you I want it. Get that paperwork ready for me before I change my mind and leave you with no commission check." I lit a cigar and waited for him to go inside and start my paperwork.

It didn't take long for it to be mine. Well, Bailee's. As a

young Black man, I took pride in knowing my credit score was in the eight hundred range and that I had bank accounts with more than three zeros behind them. On top of my accounts, I had so much money in cash that I needed to add two more safes to my collection. Yeah, I was a hood nigga by most people's standards, but I'll be damned if I lived like one.

"You're all set, Mr. Black. These are your keys. Thank you for being a part of the Mercedes Benz family." The salesman handed me the keys to Bailee's new whip but I handed them back to him.

I paid him and another salesman a hundred dollars to follow me to The Black Palace in the car. Once it was parked in the back of the building, I gave Tatianna her first assignment, which was to set up a lil' date night for me and Bailee. That would be a test for her ass too, 'cuz if she acted jealous or said anything wreckless, I was firing her on the spot and also roasting her.

"All this is for me? Domino...you didn't!" Bai exclaimed when she walked into my office, a couple of hours later.

The one thing I loved about my office was the sound proof walls. With all the noise going on outside the door, we heard nothing. It was a Saturday night, so I knew the place was lit. But it just felt like the two of us in that motherfucker.

"I did, just 'cuz you deserve that shit, Bai. You really fucking with a nigga hard, and I know you get tired of my bullshit sometime, but I appreciate you, baby. You a real one."

"Baby. Don't make me cry." She wiped her eye as a tear quickly fell. "This is beautiful."

I couldn't lie, Tatianna did her thing. And she didn't act jealous when she did it, either. She'd turned my office into a damn honeymoon suit, almost. Chocolates formatted into a large heart were on my desk, and candles and rose petals decorated the floor, leaving a trail that led to the chocolates. Since I was a nigga that loved music, I had speakers in my office, and playing was Dru Hill's "Incomplete", a fucking classic. Ironically, that song described how I felt about Bai, because although she hadn't been in my life long, I felt that if I lost her I wouldn't be complete for a while. I know I talk cash shit about not needing a bitch, but I felt like I did need her.

I took one of her hands in mine, and slid the other up her tight, short dress. She wasn't wearing any panties, which made it easier to play in her kitty cat.

"Oohh, Dommm," she cooed, feeling my thick fingers enter her opening. "I want you, baby. Right nowwwww."

"You love me?" I asked, speeding up my pace and adding another finger to her hole.

"Ye...ye...yessss."

I abruptly stopped, and then fed her the fingers that had been stroking her insides. She sopped her juices off them, and then I took her hand and led her outside.

"Why are we going outside? I wanted to finish what we started."

"We will." I promised, holding the door open for her. "I got something to show you, first."

Once we got to the car I'd purchased for her a few hours

ago, I handed her the key, which had been in my pocket. "It's yours, baby. I know you fuck with your old ride, since it belonged to your grandma and shit, but – "

"I love it, Domino! It's perfect. Thank you." She threw her arms around me and pulled me down to the ground, where I gave her the business right there on the concrete outside my club, between her new car and mine.

Chapter Five

DEDRICK BLACK

The next day...

*I*t's been a few days since I was actually introduced to Brittany by Bailee, and boy, has it been a great few days. I mean...man, this shit has been cool. I'm still trying to get the hang of all this new lingo. Between learning new slang, dressing the way Brittany likes, and fighting the urge to play with my chemicals, I didn't know which was harder. Facts. *Did I use that right?*

I just hoped all my changes were going to be worth it in the end. I think so far, they've been paying off. Brittany and I have been chatting on the phone and via text, and tonight, we were going on our first date. I rented a limousine and everything, and my driver was currently parked in the driveway waiting for me. Then, we'd go get Brittany.

I sprayed some winter fresh breath spray in my mouth,

and then blew in my hand, just to ensure that my breath was perfect. The worst thing that I could do was have bad hygiene around a girl – my brother Domino taught me that. I never realized females cared about stuff like that.

Looking in the mirror, I admired how well I'd cleaned up. The style Bailee did on my hair the night I officially met Brittany, I was still rocking. My braids on the side were put up in a small man bun. I was wearing a white short-sleeved button up shirt that I'd gotten from Macy's, along with a pair of black slacks and a pair of red loafers. I'd seen this style in a magazine, and it was starting to grow on me.

I picked up the bouquet of roses I'd ordered for Brittany off my bed, grabbed my wallet, and walked out to the limo.

"What are you doing here?"

"Nigga, you thought I was gon' let you spend an arm and a leg on a limo for a hoe? Get yo' punk ass in the backseat. I'm your driver tonight."

Domino rolled up the partition and I just laughed, wondering how in the world he knew I was renting a limo in the first place. Then it hit me – he had all of me and Davion's bank information, so he probably frequently checked our accounts.

My brother rolled down the partition and lit his cigar before pulling off. "What's the hoe's address?"

"What makes you think she's a whore?" I was dead serious – I knew she was a beautiful girl with lots of options, but I'd never heard much about her. However, I wasn't in the "in" crowd in the city of Columbia, nor at USC. So, maybe my brother knew something I didn't.

Instead of answering me, he just chuckled. "Any girl who ain't Bailee is a hoe to me. Send me the address, man."

"Did you cancel the limo, Domino? I did pay a fee to – "

"I got that shit right back and put it in my account. You wanna waste money and shit, so it's going back to me."

"How did you get a limo?"

"How is the sky blue, motherfucker? 'Cuz it just is." He blew smoke from his cigar and laughed, making a right turn on Killian Road. "I'm fucking with you, man. We have limos at the club, for the times our girls get called to dance at private parties. Always check with me before you spend some money on stupid shit. Either I already have it, or I know somebody who can get it for you."

Interesting. The rest of our trip was pretty much silent, except for the sounds of his phone going off every few minutes. I felt my palms getting sweaty as we pulled up to Brittany's house. For her family to have so much money, the house she was exiting from sure didn't reflect that.

"Are you going to open the door for her, or should I?" I unbuckled my seatbelt and asked my brother, just as we pulled into Brittany's driveway.

"I'm not opening the door for your date, nigga. I barely open the door for my own bitch."

I knew that was a lie. A blind man could see how much he'd changed since he'd met Bailee. I got out the limo just as Brittany was walking out of her front door. Holding the door open for her, I couldn't help but gawk at how beautiful she looked. She was wearing a yellow dress that showed more cleavage than I'd ever been exposed to in person. And it hugged her curves tightly, making her look like a delectable banana....and boy, did I love bananas!

"These are for you, madam." I handed the roses to her before letting her in. She accepted them and climbed into the limo, then I followed her in.

"Where the fuck y'all going? I got shit to do." Domino asked as he rolled down the partition.

"I was thinking we could go to Ruth Chris." I looked over at Brittany, who was nodded her head, letting me know she agreed with my choice in restaurants.

"Fifty dollars for a steak? That's way too much money to spend on a hoe who'll probably suck your dick if you got her something from the dollar menu. Save your coins, nigga."

My mouth fell agape, stunned by my brother's comment. Brittany rolled her eyes and flicked Domino off. "I have standards, thank you."

"Well stand 'dere and wait on the next chump to take yo' ass to Ruth Chris, 'cuz it damn sure won't be my brother. Y'all going to Cici's pizza? That shit five dollars per person, and water is free."

The crazy thing was that my brother was dead serious. Not one smirk spread across his face when he made the suggestion. He was really waiting on a response, but I was too shocked by his insults to Brittany to come up with one.

"We ain't even gotta go anywhere. Let's grab something

from Mickey D's and go back to your house." Brittany threw her thick thigh across my lap and Domino shot me a look in the mirror that said, "I told you so."

In my opinion, both of them were tripping, because I wanted to take my girl on a romantic night out. That's not how it went down, though. Imagine how crazy we probably looked, rolling up in the drive-thru in a white limousine. I guess at the end of the day where we ate didn't matter; as long as I had Brittany with me, it didn't matter to me where I was or what I was in. The more time we spent together, I started to realize that she was really the whipped to my cream. The sweet to my potato. The carbon to my dioxide. And I just wanted to show her how special she was to me...

"What do you want to do when we get to my house?" I nervously ate a fry that was way too hot, burning the roof of my mouth. *Play it cool, Dedrick. Play it cool.* I was hoping she'd want to cuddle and let me read a book to her. I wanted to read poetry to her; poetry was good for the soul. I had the perfect book at home for me to read to her, too, which was *The Collected Poems of Langston Hughes.* Either that, or *Romeo and Juliet.* Then, we could spend the night watching the sci-fi...I mean, ESPN channel.

Brittany shrugged her shoulders and sipped some of her strawberry milkshake. "I'm sure I'll think of something." She sat her milkshake in the cup holder and leaned toward me, giving me a whiff of her perfume as her breasts brushed against my shirt. I wanted to bury my face in her bosom, but I knew that was way too forward for the first date. Plus, I wouldn't have known what to do once my face was there. *Lay in it? Shake my head in them?*

I tried to concentrate on her face, but Brittany clearly had other plans. Although I was nervous about jumping the gun too soon, she quickly showed me that there was no such thing as being too forward. "You know you're sexy as hell, Dedrick. I'm sorry I never noticed you before."

"It's...it's okay." My lips trembled, sensing that she was about to lay a kiss on them. I'd never kissed a girl before. Not a real one. One on a picture, yes...

Once Brittany's lips touched mine, the fireworks in my head began to pop piercingly, and I closed my eyes tightly, hoping the kiss would last forever. It felt like it did.

"You're a pretty good kisser." Brittany took my face in her hands and caressed my cheeks. "Have you ever been intimate with a woman, Dedrick?"

I wish. "No." I said shyly, just as Domino rolled down the partition.

"Wrap that fucking dick of yours up, nigga. Hoes out here stay plotting. Fuck around and catch a disease just 'cuz you're trying to get your shit wet. And make her show you her pussy first. It's probably wrinkled and stretched out and if it is, just make her slurp you."

Slurp? I guess that's slang for fellatio.

"Don't...don't disrespect my girl, Domino!" I couldn't believe I had the courage to say that to my brother, but I couldn't let another minute go by, because who knows what he would've said next. I knew that everything he was saying had to be making Brittany uncomfortable, but I had to show her that with me, she was safe. Women liked to feel safe and secure, so I had to prove that I would have her back in every situation. "Stop...stop talking to her like that, Dom! She deserves respect."

Brittany half-smiled at me, I guess to thank me for what I'd just said to my brother. She didn't look too bothered about his remarks, but in psychology class last semester, I learned how people can hide their inner feelings when put in awkward situations.

I wrapped my arm around Brittany's neck, but she moved it to her shoulders. *I guess I did that wrong.*

"Alright, nigga. You got it. Don't call me when your dick is burning." Domino rolled the partition up and just a few minutes later, we were pulling up at home.

I opened the door, letting Brittany out first, and once Domino drove off, we went into the house. My heart raced as she grabbed my hand and asked where my bedroom was.

"It..it...it's there." I pointed to my closed door.

I hadn't planned on having her come here, so I didn't exactly clean up my room, but she didn't mind. She moved the lab coats off my bed and took a seat on the bed, then pulled me on top of her.

I felt my penis rising steadily as her gentle arms locked around me, and she began whispering softly in my ear. "Give it to me, Dedrick."

If only I knew how...

Brittany didn't wait for me to act – she began unbuttoning my pants and released my snack, which was growing by the second. "Pretty big. Just like I like 'em."

She seemed impressed.

Taking my large pole in her hand, Brittany rolled on top of me and bent down to put my penis – *dick,* that's the cool word – in her mouth, and just seconds after feeling her warm saliva on the head, corona, and shaft, I shot out my semen. I thought Brittany would be angry with me for getting it all in her mouth, but she swallowed it and then asked for more. Since I couldn't guarantee that I had more at the moment, I remained silent, while Brittany continued sucking. Pretty soon, my dick went from a gummy worm to hard again, swelling and filling her mouth. She took my balls in her mouth, and they felt like Silly Putty as they were being swallowed by her jaws.

After giving my man parts a few more minutes of action, Brittany came up for air and pushed me onto my bed. I didn't have to do any of the work – she eagerly hopped on top of me and began opening her vaginal lips to place on my manhood.

"Whooaaa." I gasped, upon feeling myself enter into the unknown garden of womanhood for the first time.

So this is what it feels like?!

I bit my lip, trying not to blurt out a proposal, because that's how good sexual contact with Brittany felt. Her insides were so moist, and although I didn't want to be offensive, I began hollering out obscenities as she rocked her hips back and forth on me. The same intense feeling that I'd felt every night that I masturbated, I was feeling now, but it was much better since I had the girl of my dreams in person, versus in a picture. I couldn't believe I'd waited so long in life to feel this, but I was ecstatic that it was with Brittany. I will love her forever.

Chapter Six

DAVION "BABY D" BLACK

s I sat in my running car outside of the locker room, I was tempted as fuck to turn around and go either back to my dorm or to the crib. I needed a fucking hit. Well, another hit, considering the fact that I was already high. I had to calm my nerves before I walked into this motherfucker, and now that I was here, I felt like I needed just a little bit more.

The assistant coach and offense coach hit me up about a meeting, and since I had just come from a lawyer's office, I was aggravated as fuck. All them niggas could suck my dick honestly, because they knew damn well that had I known Shanay was a kid, I wouldn't have looked her way. When I met with the lawyer not too long ago, she showed me proof that Shanay was indeed fourteen, and pregnant. The birth certificate confirmed her age, and an ultrasound proved the pregnancy. But, that still didn't mean the baby was mine. Just like Camiyah was gon' have to show me a paternity test, Shanay would too. But honestly, I didn't want or need a baby with a fucking freshman in high school, so my plan was to push her down the stairs or something. I just haven't figured out how I'm going to get to her yet. But I had to kill the little fuck.

Checking my Rolex, I saw that it was seven o'clock, which meant if I walked in right now, I'd be right on time. Since motherfuckers moved on my time and not theirs, I sat in my whip for an extra five minutes, then got out. If they knew what was good for them, they'd still be waiting for me whether I went in now or in two hours.

"Davion. Glad you could finally join us."

I was only six minutes late.

The assistant coach motioned toward a seat on the opposite side of the table from where they were sitting. "Have a seat, Mr. Black."

Ignoring them niggas, I asked, "Where's Coach Starkes?" I wasn't looking for him necessarily, but I did think it was quite pussy of him to not face me. After all, he had enough balls to have hit me. Shit, I still had plans on fucking him up. Maybe it was best that he wasn't here, for his sake.

"Coach Starkes is actually who we'll be talking about. He didn't want to be in attendance...for...obvious reasons." The offense coach, Coach Cannon, cleared his throat and then folded his hands like he was praying. That pussy motherfucker better be praying my foot didn't land up his ass, 'cuz that's exactly what's going to happen if he said some foul shit to me.

Biting my bottom lip, which was a trait I'd picked up as a young nigga when I knew shit was about to hit the fan, I asked, "What's this lil' pow wow about? I got shit to do."

"Yeah, well I know one thing. You won't be having a damn thing to do with this team if you keep that fucking attitude."

I jumped up out my seat, ready to maul Coach Cannon like the bitch he was. But, Coach Brown rushed over to me and pushed me back down in my chair. These niggas did not know who the fuck I was, because if they did, they would tread real lightly...

"I *am* this damn team, and I ain't even started playing yet." I laughed and ran my hand over my waves. "Now like I said, what y'all need to discuss with me? Y'all wasting my fucking time and energy."

"Coach Starkes is leaving, Davion." Coach Brown blurted out, causing a smile to spread across my face. "He's resigning. We called you here to tell you, but also to warn you that if anything else like this ever happens again, you'll never catch a football again."

"And if I can't catch a football, I'll catch your wife's cum in my mouth," I spat, pissing that nigga off.

He turned red as a tomato, but all he did was laugh and shake his head. "That mouth and that attitude of yours...son, you're not going far."

"I know where I'm going right now, though." I stood up and pushed the chair in. Chucking the deuces at them, I laughed and said, "I'm out." Niggas tried to hold me back, but as always, I would come out on top.

*O*ne *hour later...*
I hit Celine up a couple of times, but shorty wasn't answering the phone for me. I wanted to talk to her because during the times we kicked it, she seemed cool, for the most part. I wanted to be around someone who wouldn't judge me, since it seemed like everybody was against me all of a sudden.

After trying to call the bitch about seven times, I finally came to the conclusion that she was avoiding me 'cuz of all that shit that had gone done with Shanay and Camiyah; both incidents made the news. But, Celine couldn't think for one minute she was gon' just get away from me. See, bitches didn't let me go, I let them go. And I wasn't quite finished with her. So, if she didn't want to answer my calls, she'd just be answering the fucking door for me.

"What are you doing here, Davion? Don't you have some-body else to go bother, puto?" Celine folded her arms across her sexy ass breasts and tried to walk away from me. But, I grabbed her by the tiny ass waist and brought her closer to me.

"I want you, Celine. Let me in."

"Your breath smells like beer and smoke! I don't want you in here! No Bueno!"

"I don't give a fuck what you want, bitch." I tried to kiss

her, but she ducked, so I grabbed her face and squeezed her lil' cute, plump cheeks. "You don't want me, Celine? That's what you're saying?" Before the dumb bitch had the nerve to say some stupid shit to me, I squeezed her cheeks tighter, making her face turn red. Shorty had me fucked up, disrespecting me like I was just anybody. "I am not one of those whack ass niggas you're used to, bitch! Nobody is fucking playing with you!"

Tears fell from her pretty ass face, but I knew she was just trying to punk me. Only a soft motherfucker would fall for that shit.

"Fuck is you crying for, girl? I'm trying to fuck you!" I let her face go, only 'cuz I wanted her jaws sucking my joint within the next few minutes. I tried to push her head toward my dick, but she escaped my damn grip. Strong ass.

"That's the problem, Davion! You're thinking with your dick, papi, and not your cabeza! I ignored what everybody said about you, but you haven't changed one bit! Now on the news I see you've got a baby coming with a young chica, and another girl was shot at your house! Was it the same girl who keyed my car?" She laughed like a fucking maniac, then shook her head. "It probably was, Davion. You don't want a good woman. You want someone who's gonna put up with your shit, but that's not me. Not anymore. Eres vergonzoso. Before you ask, it means you're embarrassing, papi."

I laughed, 'cuz she was the one who was gon' be embarrassed. She must not have realized, I was Davion Motherfucking Black. I think I sweated her too much and gave her the big head, but she was sadly mistaken if she thought I needed her. I just wanted her 'cuz the pussy and head was good, and a nigga loved to hear that lil' Spanish accent when I was balls deep. Otherwise, she could step just like the rest of these hoes. She was gon' need me before I needed her. Bet.

"Fuck you, Celine-Wish-You-Were-Selena." I punched her front door so hard she started shaking. That bitch had better watch her back. She was on my shit list and hit list now, talking to me like she didn't have no goddamn sense.

A few hours later... Since that lil' Spanish bitch wanted to piss me off, I found a cheap hoe on a corner to fuck with. I got us some smoke and a room at fucking cheap ass motel, so I could get my high and bust my nut in peace. Even though I've been in the news lately, motherfuckers around Columbia still bowed down to me. With that being said, I got not only some coke for free, but I also got this run-down room for free. I was only staying here long enough to bust this hoe down, so I didn't care how tacky it was.

"What's your name again?" I asked the hoe, after I snorted a line. "Nevermind. You took too long to answer. Suck my dick, yo."

She got down on her knees, and took my snake out my pants, then wrapped her lips around it. She was acting like she was scared of it.

"I know it's big," I laughed, blowing out smoke from the blunt I'd just rolled. "But it don't bite. Suck that shit."

She opened her mouth wider, but she still was acting like she was scared to take me in fully. I was gon' help her with that shit, though, or this would be one hoe who did not get paid tonight.

Palming the back of her head, I pushed her mouth further onto my dick, then when she started to get into the rhythm, I pulled that fucking horrible pink wig off. She looked like a damn troll, or like a bottle of Pepto Bismol. "That wig was the fucking problem. It was in the way, bitch. Suck that shit the right way, or I'll send you back to the corner with no bread."

Now that her wig was off, she was getting her ass to work. Right before I felt myself about to bust, I pushed her off me so I could slip a condom on my jimmy and beat her from the back. Doggy style was the only way I was fucking her, 'cuz her face wasn't cute enough for me to want to look at.

After I finished popping her off, she asked if she could stay the night, and the only reason I let her was because I would probably be wanting some more head whenever I woke up. I lit another blunt and checked my phone as she fell asleep, and I saw Camiyah had been blowing my shit up. I texted her to tell her to chill the fuck out because I was getting my dick wet, then blocked her number.

I called Celine, but the bitch didn't answer. So, I sent her a picture of my dick, to show her what the fuck she was missing out on. When she didn't respond the way I wanted her to, I sent her messages back to back, cursing her simple ass out. I didn't know if she was stupid, slow, or just plain fucking ignorant, but she was lucky I didn't drive over to that ugly ass townhouse and beat her the fuck up. I wanted the bitch bad, but I wanted my respect more. Everybody in the city...fuck, the *nation,* gave ya boy respect, 'cuz I did numbers on that football field. Here comes this Spanish bitch, treating me like I was some regular nigga. I might call Trump to deport her ass.

Celine wouldn't respond to any of my messages, so I finally laid my shit on the dresser, slipped on another condom, and rolled over on top of the hoe bitch. She was laying in the perfect position – on her stomach – so I still didn't have to look at that busted up face. Bitch looked like a boogawolf, but that pussy was wet, and that was all I gave a fuck about.

The next morning...
        I woke up, reaching out for lil' ugly, so I could hit it one last time before I sent her back to the streets. But, there was nobody in the bed with me.

I jumped up to see a note on the dresser that read, "Thanks". When I noticed my wallet was missing, I realized exactly what she was thanking me for.

I couldn't believe that two dollar hoe robbed me, but I guess it was my karma, 'cuz I wasn't gon' pay her ass anyway, since she started off with giving me mediocre head. Or if I did pay her, I wasn't giving her the full amount she'd asked for. That top wasn't worth a hundred, and neither was that stretched ass pussy. I know one thing – if I ever saw her out on the streets, I was blowing her head off. On sight.

Checking my phone, I saw where Shanay had hit me up, saying she'd moved out of state and wanted to talk to me. I blocked that bitch's number right away, 'cuz if I responded, it wasn't gon' be pretty at all. Then, her punk ass pops would probably be calling the pigs on me again, and I wasn't trying to feel that.

Chapter Seven

CELINE GOMEZ

$\mathcal{D}$uring the entire twenty-four-hour day yesterday, Davion stressed me the hell out. Completely. From the visit to my place, to the late-night calls and texts... he was bugging. El es realmente loco...

I know people think I'm out of my cabeza for dealing with him, and that's because I probably was. At one point, I was stuck on Davion, but now I'm starting to see that I can't help him. He's got problems...muchos problemas...and I refuse to be used as his punching bag any longer.

See, I lost my brother, Arturo, a few years ago. The same way Davion is behaving is the same way Arturo used to behave. The drugs got him. He used to threaten the familia, steal money from us...all the things Davion does, Arturo used to do. One day, he overdosed, and I hated myself for not trying to reach out to him before it got to the point it did.

When I met Davion at The Black Palace on el Cuatro de Julio, I didn't know he came with so many problems. After his true colors, I decided to help him, because if I could save at least one life, maybe Arturo's wouldn't have gone in vain. But, the disrespect from Davion has gotten much worse, and I can't take it anymore. I liked him, but I didn't like him more than I liked myself.

A *few hours later...*

Since Rhyan had moved out of the townhouse, my neighbor had been using her room for extra storage. They were really cool, so when they asked, it wasn't a big deal. One of the girls who lived beside me named Erica explained that she had a brother, Eric, who had lost his house in a fire a few weeks ago, so the belongings he wanted to salvage were the ones in the room.

Today, he was coming to get them, because he'd found an apartment to move into, according to Erica. I heard the doorbell ring just as I was putting my floss back in my medicine cabinet.

I ran down the stairs to open the door, and when I did, I was looking at a beautiful man. *Muy guapo...*

"Hi. Are you Celine?" He asked, flashing a smile that advertised thirty-two of the whitest teeth I'd ever seen. Wearing a tight red ribbed shirt that hugged his muscles, and a pair of dark black denim jeans, he looked like a cherry dipped in chocolate. His hair was neatly cut, and his beard was trimmed nicely, too. If Morris Chestnut had a younger twin, it would be him.

Snapping from my thoughts, I nodded my head. "Sí. I'm Celine. Are you Eric?"

"Yes. Thanks for housing my things. I want to give you something, just as a token of appreciation." He reached in his pocket to grab his wallet. He pulled out three twenty-dollar bills, but I tried to decline them. Eric wouldn't let me, though. "Take it, please. It's not a lot, and that's because at this moment, I don't have a lot. But, I just want to thank you for your hospitality. You didn't have to let me use your extra room."

Reluctantly, I took the money from his hand and thanked him. He had me so in shock, because he was not only appealing to the eye, but he seemed to be nice as well.

"Come on in." I opened the door to let him in. "Your stuff is in the room on the left."

Eric made several trips to and from his car, carrying boxes and bags of his belongings. Each time I offered to help, he thanked me but declined my offer. "Not saying I don't want you to touch my things or anything," he laughed. "But, I just don't believe it's a woman's job to lift a finger. I got it."

"Well, what is a woman's job?" I was curious to know his thoughts. I hoped it wasn't one of those old school answers, like 'to be barefoot and pregnant'. That would be such a turn off.

Showing the dimples he had on both sides, Eric smiled. "It's a woman's job to be loved by her man. I think that's all a woman's job is. To let her man honor her, love her, respect her, and take care of her."

My knees buckled upon hearing his answer, because it wasn't what I was expecting. After dealing with Davion, hearing a man like Eric speak on women in a good light was like a breath of fresh air. I nodded my head and smiled, to let him know I loved his answer.

Once everything was cleared out of the room, I didn't want him to leave. So, I offered to cook for him.

"Damn. You're beautiful, you're hospitable, and you cook too? I might just have to call my mama and let her know I found the one."

Yeah, you should.

"Make yourself comfortable. I'll put on some arroz con pollo. Do you eat chicken and rice?" I handed him the remote to the TV in the den as he took a seat on my couch.

"I do. Thank you."

Once I washed my hands, I got to work in the kitchen. I was a pretty good cook, if I do say so myself, so I was sure Eric would enjoy the lunch I was preparing. I made sure I did as my abuela always did when she cooked for a man, and made his food with love. I was hoping this wouldn't be the last I saw of him.

Chapter Eight

BAILEE RODGERS

A few days later...

*L*ife has been such an emotional rollercoaster for me lately. I didn't know whether I was coming or going lately, and I hated the way my mood swings affected my relationship with Dom.

I know it sounds crazy, because some people may think I should be over it by now, but the fact that Tyler raped me was still fucking with me...hard. Some days I was okay, and others all I did was think about it. Flashbacks of his scrawny, sweaty, behind forcing himself on top of me played in my mind, over and over again. Even when I closed my eyes and tried my hardest to think about Domino, the man I loved, Tyler's evil face would appear. I thought I was going fucking insane.

"What's going on with you, Bail? You're acting all quiet and shit. Like you're mad at a nigga or something. What the fuck did I do now?" Domino slid his hand up and down my thigh, which would've normally aroused me and made me blush. But right now, I just wanted his hands off my body.

"Don't touch me, Dom." I removed his hand from my thigh and put it back on the steering wheel.

"I don't know what the fuck your problem is, Bailee Rodgers, but you'd better fix your fucking attitude before I fix it for you. You got a nigga acting right and shit, and now you wanna trip? You lucky I love yo' ass, 'cuz with the way you been acting today, I should've been let another bitch sit on my dick."

"Oh, like Tatianna?" I spat, rolling my neck and eyes so hard I thought they were going to disconnect from my body.

Yesterday, his phone was going off like a drug dealer's, and I let curiosity get the best of me for whatever reason. I didn't go in his phone, but I did tap the home screen and saw that he had texts from a girl named Tatianna. He'd never mentioned a Tatianna before, so it felt like he was hiding something. Tierra, Sapphire, now Tatianna...this man's list was a mile long and I could only feel slightly insecure about where my place was. I couldn't help but think that my time with him would be up soon.

I expected him to be mad at the fact that I'd done some snooping, because most niggas hated having their privacy invaded, especially when they were up to something. But instead, Domino flashed a wide smile, showing all of his thirty-two perfect teeth. As he made a left on Carter Street, he asked, "So, you were going through my phone? You found anything?"

"Should I have? And I didn't go through your phone, Domino."

"Save it. You ain't the first bitch I've been with, so I know y'all motherfuckers are nosey. The only difference is I used to delete shit when I was with Sapphire, 'cuz I was actually doing something. I ain't fucking around on you and if I was baby girl, trust me, you'd never know. Tatianna works for me. I hired her to take Sherita's place. The same broad you asked me about when she was coming out the club a few days ago. Don't nobody want no loose pussy Tatianna, alright? 'Cuz if I was trying to fuck with her, her name would be saved as Todd or some shit."

He said that shit like this was okay. It wasn't. Not only was I now wondering if all the niggas in his phone were code names for females, but I was mad as hell that he never told me he'd hired a new manager for The Black Palace. I told him I could run the place, but he told me he wanted me to focus on cosmetology school. Now it felt like that was his excuse for having to hire a bitch like Tatianna, who had the body of the strippers she was going to manage, and a beautiful face to match.

Usually my self-esteem wasn't this low. I felt like shit. Domino was supposed to be my safe haven, but I didn't even want to be around him right now. "When we get to my parents' house, just drop me off. Don't you dare get out of your car."

"Or what, Bailee? What the fuck are you gonna do if I get

out at your parents' crib? After all, that's what they're expecting me to do, anyway."

Since I'd already dropped my fall classes and was planning to enroll at the Kenneth Shuler School of Cosmetology, I figured I might as well drop the bomb on my parents that I was moving in with Domino. Just to win my dad's support with everything, I decided to invite Domino for dinner tonight at their house. And now that we were less than ten minutes away, I was regretting everything. The move. The relationship. Everything.

"I'm just not ready for this Domino." I tilted my head, so my eyes were staring at my lap, and luckily Domino was driving, so he didn't see the tears that decorated my cheeks.

I wished I could tell him that the way I was feeling really had nothing to do with him – more so with my hurt, shame, and disgust from what Tyler did to me. I don't know, I've been reading articles and forums online from rape victims, and they all said that a person didn't get over the pain and depression until they faced it head on. I wasn't that strong yet, though. I couldn't face Tyler. Seeing him in my dreams – well nightmares – was hard enough.

"You're not ready for what, Bailee? You're not ready to be with me? All this shit – it was for nothing?"

I opened my mouth to tell him that I was sorry and didn't mean it, but no words came out. And since I was silent, he just nodded his head as he parked in my parents' driveway. I unbuckled my seatbelt, which was something Domino would always handle for me. Once I got out of the car, and I saw he wasn't getting out with me, I got even angrier. It's like, I wanted to tell him but then again I didn't...

"Fine, Domino. Act like that." I didn't even know what I was referring to, because he wasn't doing anything wrong. But at this point, I just wanted to be alone.

He opened his mouth to speak, but instead, he just chuckled and shook his head. "Get at me when you're ready, baby. I'm too old to be playing motherfucking games." He backed out of my parents' driveway, leaving me feeling helpless and alone.

Two days later...
This was the longest I'd gone without speaking to Domino, and I felt sick. Literally sick to my stomach. I was an Aquarius and he was a Leo, so we were both stubborn as hell. I hadn't called him, and surprisingly, he hadn't called me. I had typed out about fifty different texts to send to him, just to delete them all.

I'd been moping around the house, and the fact that my parents constantly questioned me about why they didn't meet him for dinner the other night wasn't helping. I made up some bullshit excuse about him having an emergency at work to pacify my mother, but my dad knew me well enough to know I was lying. I think he was the one that genuinely wanted to meet him; my mom probably only wanted to meet him so she'd have some shit to talk down on me about.

Today, I'd finally decided to take my ass down to Kenneth

Shuler to enroll in my cosmetology classes. I had confided in my parents about dropping my fall classes, and although my mom was heated...I mean heated − because she felt like I was wasting her money, my knowledge, and everything else − I felt confident I was doing the right thing. My dad was proud of the fact that I was chasing my dreams, just as he'd done. People like my mom chased money, which was cool, but I'll be damned if I was a nurse with a stack of money, unhappy as hell, every day.

I got up from my bed for what seemed like the first time in years, and went into the bathroom to finally shower, brush my teeth, and get dressed. One thing I always tried to make sure of was that my outside appearance didn't reflect the inside, so although I felt like pure shit, I got cute. Real cute.

I loved the color black against my skin. My complexion was so rich and milk chocolate that black complemented it well. So, I threw on a black tube dress, a pair of low top black and white vans, and put my hair in a huge bun. After applying my MAC red lipstick, I grabbed my Brahmin bag and headed out the door.

Nothing made me happier than stepping into the Kenneth Shuler School of Cosmetology for the first time. I was greeted by this beautiful woman, with flawless makeup and hair, who showed me around the campus. She explained that I'd only need less than a year to be licensed in the state of South Carolina, and that after that, I was free to work in any shop around town, instead of being a kitchen beautician. I had other plans, though. I wanted to open a shop. At one point,

Domino was the one who was going to help me with that, but I was a strong woman, so I'd have no problem figuring out shit on my own.

Speaking of Dom, he was the reason I was here right now. Not only had he pushed me to pursue my dream, but he'd given me a blank check sometime last week, so that when I was ready to enroll, he could pay for my classes. I felt bad about the fact that I was now about to use it, but I didn't think he was an Indian giver.

"Thank you, Bailee. You're all set for your classes to begin next week." Kim, the enrollment counselor, smiled as she shook my hand and gave me a folder filled with information about the program I'd just become a part of. "Welcome to the Kenneth Shuler family."

With tears in my eyes, I replied, "Thank you."

She gave me another quick tour of the school, showed me the bookstore where I could purchase some materials, and then told me I was free to go. Not that I really wanted to leave – I was enjoying my time here. But, I was ready to leave so I could share the news with my dad. He was the only person I felt would be genuinely happy for my new journey. Except...

"Domino? What are you doing here?" I rolled my eyes like I was irritated, but inside I was grinning from ear to ear.

He was standing there, looking like a Mr. Goodbar with *all* the nuts, wearing a tight, yellow Balmain shirt with black jeans. The sight of Domino's muscles bulging from his shirt and the undeniable thick dick print through his jeans made me want to wrap my legs around his face and ride it, but I constrained myself. After all, he was no longer my man...or was he?

"Bailee. You know me better than that. You know anywhere my checks get cashed, that's where I'm gonna be."

Damn. The enrollment counselor chick at Kenneth Shuler didn't waste much time processing my money, if he was able to track it. I knew his bank app alerted him anytime a change was made to his account, so no wonder he was able to find me.

"Go away." I turned back around and could barely take one step before feeling his hand grab mine.

"I don't know what the fuck you got going on, but here's the deal. You either my bitch or I'm yo' nigga. You feel me?"

No. That shit didn't make any sense.

I guess he noticed my confusion, because he just laughed. "Basically you either mine 'cuz you wanna be or you mine 'cuz I want you to be. Which one is it?"

I laughed, because I hoped this moment would come. I wanted him to come find me, and demand that I be with him. "I'm with you because I wanna be, Domino."

"And don't bitch. Just be my bitch. Alright?"

Rolling my eyes, I smiled as he placed a light kiss on my lips. I whispered, "I'm sorry" as he gently massaged my ass while kissing me.

"It's cool. I'll punish you for it later."

Freaky ass...

. . .

L *ater that night...*
        My first impression of Tatianna was that she was just another little whore trying to throw her pussy at my man. But now that I was watching her and Domino crunch numbers in his office, I was able to see that she was about her business. And I could appreciate that.

"I'm sick of looking at numbers, now. I wanna look at some ass. I'm out." Domino rose from his seat and Tatianna and I followed suit.

They'd been discussing the budget for The Black Palace, and she was trying to convince him to hire vendors for certain products, such as uniforms for the dancers, and liquor and food. I could tell he wasn't really feeling it, though, because Domino wasn't one that liked restrictions. And of course, if he were to sign a contract with a vendor, he was stuck. But, Tatianna showed him on paper how much money they'd save if they did it that way.

"When will you be able to let me know something, Mr. Black? I told everyone I'd get back to them next week." The emphasis she put on his name made me want to open my mouth to go off, but I didn't. Maybe she didn't mean it...it just sounded like she was stressing it the same way a bitch would in the bedroom. I didn't like it.

"You can get back to them whenever the fuck you feel like it. I ain't getting back to you 'til I want to, though. And I'm 98% sure the same "no" I'm thinking is the one you'll get when you ask me again."

Dom grabbed my hand and after Tatianna walked out of

his office, we walked out too. When we got to the VIP section, there was a surprise of a lifetime waiting for us. Janay was sitting on Weezy's lap, giving him a dance so sensual that they were practically fucking with their clothes on. I let them finish, but as soon as Chris Brown's "Strip" went off, I was in my girl's ass.

"Janay! You do know he's married, right?"

She shrugged her shoulders and laughed. Domino shot me a look that said, "*I told you your friends are hoes.*" Ignoring him, I focused my attention back on my girl, who was happily bouncing away on that married fucking man.

I mean, since Janay danced for niggas as a side gig, I wouldn't have really tripped about it, had this been a random. But the fact that she was just dancing at his birthday party and now all out in the open with this nigga made me feel like it was something more. I know if Dom was letting a bitch do that on him, I would be beating ass from here to Africa. So I could only imagine how his wife felt.

"I'm separated at the moment, so you can mind your motherfucking business, bitch." Weezy didn't even get a chance to finish insulting me before Domino was in his face. He took the bottle of Budweiser he was drinking from his hand and cracked it over his head.

"Oh my God!" Janay screamed, as the glass and beer splattered everywhere, including on her, since she was right beside his disrespectful ass.

"I'll crack another one over your motherfucking head if you got some shit to say." Domino threatened Janay, holding the broken bottle. "Get y'all's funky asses out my club. Smelling like toilet water and spoiled milk."

Dom was loud as hell and had caused a scene, so everybody in the club was laughing at their expense. I could tell Janay was embarrassed, but oh well. I tried to worn her.

When Weezy was finally able to stand up, there was blood coming down his face, but like the druggie he was, he just laughed. "You've changed, nigga. Don't let a bitch make you forget who you really fuck with. Shit, I'll be here when you get tired of her and want something new."

"And Lena will be here when you least expect it." Domino shot back, pointing to the door where Weezy's big ass wife was coming in. This was my first time seeing her in person, and I almost felt bad for Weezy because she was so much bigger than him.

I got out of the way fast, because although home girl was on the big and tall side, she was quick on her feet. She damn near flew over to the spot we were at, just to jack Weezy up by his collar.

"I told you! Stop coming to this damn club with these damn stripper bitches, Renard Archibald Wright! You must want me to put my foot in your ass! Come on home!"

Damn. She pulled out the government name.

The entire club erupted in laughter as Lena literally carried Weezy out like he was a baby – bridal style. Janay left right after them, without saying goodbye or even looking my way. I guess she was embarrassed too, but I don't know why. I told her that man was married, and she seemed to not give a fuck.

It felt like I was losing so many people over my relationship with Domino, but when I was younger, my grandma used to tell me that sometimes God weeded out people for you. Wrapped in Domino's strong arms was where I was supposed to be, and no one could convince me differently. And if anybody didn't like it, in the words of my man, "fuck 'em."

*T**he next day...***
My sister texted me asking if we could meet up for drinks, and although Tas was one of the last people I wanted to see, I told her to meet me at Ruby's, which was a bar not too far from Domino's crib, at five o'clock. Since it was almost four thirty now, I was about to leave his house.

"Where you going, looking all sexy? You look like you want me to put a baby in you or something." Domino stuck his tongue down my throat and massaged my ass gently.

I was wearing an orange tube dress, and I'll admit, it did hug my curves in all the right areas, so I wasn't surprised that he had a hard-on. I reached for his dick through his grey sweatpants and rubbed it. "I'll take care of you when I get back. I promise."

"Where you going now? I'll probably head to the club soon."

"Just to Ruby's to meet my sister. I'll be back in a few."

Instead of responding, Domino nodded and gave me a kiss on my forehead. He went in his pocket and handed me his American Express card. "Don't wild the fuck out, now. But have a nice dinner." He slapped me on the ass as I walked past him, grabbing my brown Michael Kors Brooklyn bag from the coatrack.

When I walked into Ruby's, I spotted my sister waiting for me at the bar. She'd already ordered what appeared to be a Long Island Iced Tea, and when I sat down, I ordered the same.

Sitting beside her was so awkward. We hadn't been fucking with each other at *all* lately, so I was curious as to why she felt compelled to invite me for dinner and drinks. "What's going on, Tasmine? Everything okay?"

"Everything with me is great. Everything with you...I'm not sure."

Really? Everything with me was just fine.

"What the fuck does that mean?" I accepted the drink from the bartender, stirred it up a bit, and then began sipping, waiting on her dumb ass response. When she didn't say anything, I repeated my question. "What the fuck does that mean, Tasmine?"

"I think you're being brainwashed, Bailee! Domino...he's not good for you at all. He's got a baby on the way. And he's cheating on you. Why can everybody see this but you?"

Baby? Cheating? This bitch had my man fucked up...

"Tasmine. I love you, okay? But you must be talking about another Domino Black, because the one I'm in love with never."

Tasmine rolled her eyes and handed me her phone, which was already showing an Instagram page for that Tierra chick that wouldn't leave Domino alone. Out of curiosity I took the phone from my sister and began to scroll through her pictures, and sure enough, on each one, her hand was on top of her almost non-existent belly, and the caption referenced "Baby Black".

But, what did that prove? Nothing more than Domino had already told me and what I already knew. Tierra was a desperate female who would do anything to keep a man, including fake a pregnancy. Not saying she was faking, but I felt that until she was proven right, Domino couldn't be proven wrong.

I handed Tasmine her phone and before I could utter another word, I suddenly fell ill at the sight before me. If you've ever been in a situation where you literally couldn't believe your eyes, then you would understand.

"Did you have anything to do with them coming here?" I asked Tasmine, as I pointed to the duo who'd just walked through the doors, Rhyan and Tyler.

The worst part about it was that they were holding hands. I wanted to across the room and chop their hands off. Rhyan was taking disrespecting me to a whole 'nother level, and the sight of Tyler made me want to vomit because of what he'd done to me. A flood of emotions, ranging from angry to hurt to scared, rushed through my body, and all I wanted to do was watch him get raped, so he would see how it felt to have his body violated. But instead of running over there where they were walking and acting out, I looked the other way and began to cry. Not because I was jealous, because I didn't want shit to do with Tyler, but because I felt so betrayed. By everyone, including my sister.

Tas turned around and shook her head almost immediately. "I had no idea they'd be here together. If you want to leave, we can leave."

I didn't know if I should believe her or not. Until recently, I'd never thought my sister would be the type to try to hurt me, but all her moves were shady to me. She was so anti-Domino that I was starting to believe she wanted him herself. Either that, or she was just hating on what we had because she was so unhappy with her life. Landon wasn't exactly a prize...

"I don't need to leave, Tasmine." I responded, taking a sip of my drink. "I can sit in the presence of my enemies without being affected. After all, I've beat that ass once. I can do it again." I said that shit loudly enough for Rhyan and Tyler to both hear me. Tyler ignored me, but I could tell I'd embarrassed Rhyan.

I then focused my attention back to my sister after the bartender brought me another Long Island Iced Tea. "Thanks for trying to look out, if that's what you were really doing. But I know exactly who that bitch is in the pictures. And she's crazy. Trust me, Domino does not have a baby on the way."

I didn't know who I was trying to convince, her or myself. That Tierra chick was crazy as hell, but she could very well be carrying my man's baby. I wasn't sure. I would hope that if she was, he would be the one to tell me and not my sister.

"Okay, Bailee. I hope I'm wrong. I just...I just want what's best for you. And I don't see Domino being it."

"Well open your eyes, sis. Because he is. To the world, he's this mean, arrogant, violent nigga, but to me he's sweet, caring, and protective. I couldn't ask for anything else." I finished my drink without saying another word to her about Domino. While I was sitting there, I could feel both Rhyan's and Tyler's eyes on me, and I couldn't wait to get back to my man to tell him about all this bullshit that went down.

s soon as I got in the car with Lena last night, her stupid ass slapped the fuck out of me, leaving me with the black eye I was currently nursing a day later in our basement, which used to be my mancave but was now my punishment room. Lena didn't like the idea of me having a spot where I could relax and shit, so she took everything from out of here, leaving me with nothing but a goddamn folding chair and bathroom. My mancave used to be the spot for me and my boys; I had pool table, a mini fridge, and a fifty-inch TV. I also had a couch with a pullout bed in case any of those motherfuckers decided to stay the night so they wouldn't drive drunk. But when I lost my job, Lena went on trip mode and put a nigga on major lock down.

I wished I had somebody to talk to, man, about all the shit that goes down at 323 Grimwell Street. My niggas thought I was just another smoked out, cheating motherfucker, but that wasn't the case. I mean, shit, that *was* the case, but there was a reason behind all my madness. I smoked and popped pills because every high numbed all the pain I felt on the regular. Truth be told, that's how Baby D got wrapped into all my fucking mess – I told him how I ease my mind with my pills, needles, and weed, and that lil' nigga dug in.

See, when I was just a lil' nigga, fresh out of my father's ball sack, he started beating the fuck out of my mom. I later found out he was on that shit and honestly couldn't help it, but that didn't make it any better. My dad used to fuck my mom up, yo. Dragging by her hair, knocking her in the face... all that shit. Seeing how fucked up my pops always had my mom's face looking, I told myself I'd never put my hands on a woman. It's ironic as fuck that the same shit I didn't want to do a bitch, was the same shit a

bitch was doing to me.

Don't get me wrong, man, a nigga was far from perfect, but did I deserve to be slapped around by my motherfucking wife every day? Nah. And to be honest, she was really only mad at herself, because she knew damn well them kids weren't mine. I cheated on her a few times, back in the day, so then she did the shit to me. The thing is, she got pregnant from her lil' affair. She guilted me into taking her back, which I did, but I wished like fuck I hadn't.

I didn't have the proof that her kids weren't mine, but shit, the lil' niggas took none of my features. Jayden was big as hell, just like Lena, with brown skin and big eyes like her too.

By next year the lil' motherfucker would be bigger than me. Kayden had my skin complexion and my eyes, but all her mama's tendencies. She was bossy and mean, and although I'd been raising her and Jay like they were my own all these years, I was ready to pack my shit up and leave all of 'em here. It was either that or I was gon' fuck around and kill Lena.

After I finished icing my eye, I decided to pull out my iPhone X and hit up Janay. I wanted to check on baby girl since Lena had to show her ass at the club the other night. Like a lil' nervous bitch ass nigga, I waited for the indication that Janay had read my message, but she never responded. Fuck, I'd probably lost her before I'd gotten her. With any other female, I wouldn't have given a fuck, but something about Janay had me intrigued from the jump. I hated the thought of her not wanting anything to do with me.

I met Janay a few weeks ago, when she danced for me at my birthday party. Roman booked her; he knew her because they fucked around for maybe a day or two, but they lost interest in one another. Roman was like that, though. He didn't hold on to females long. Me...I wanted to see what she was about.

We kept in contact 'cuz shorty was cute as fuck and could throw her ass back like a pro, and also because she seemed down to fucking earth. We had a lot of similarities – both of us had too many responsibilities and not enough money.

I didn't even ask her to fuck me after she danced. I knew she would have, since she needed the bread, but instead, I just gave her the last lil' bit I had. I wanted to fuck with her, but not just for a night. I don't know man...I'm twenty-nine-years-old, and other than a reputation in the streets as a nigga whose bitch had him on lock, I didn't have shit going for myself. I couldn't keep a job 'cuz of my drug habit, and I couldn't kick the habit because of the shit I dealt with at home.

"Renard! I hope your stupid, punk ass is down there thinking about what the fuck you did!" I heard Lena yelling from the top floor of our basement. "If you're not, I'm coming down there to show you who you won't be playing with, cheating, broke, motherfucker! Sorry ass bitch! I'll give you another eye to match the one I gave you! You're about as useless as the ice cream machine at McDonald's, since your ass ain't never working!"

See? Shit like that would break a nigga's spirits down, even if he was trying to be on the straight on and narrow. That's why I didn't fucking try anymore. Not with finding a job, not with being a faithful husband, or even a good dad...or step-dad...shit, whatever I was...

When I heard the door to what was supposed to be our, but was really just Lena's bedroom slam, I decided to do what I did at least twice a week, which was escape out the window. Some nights, I found a cheap hooker walking the streets to hook up with, and others, I slept on benches and shit like a homeless-ass nigga, just so I wouldn't have to be under the same roof as Lena. Today, I had plans of going to see Janay. She hadn't texted me back yet, but I was determined to see her fine-ass and apologize for Lena's behavior last night at the club. I mean, shorty knew I was married because I'm an honest-ass nigga. But, she also knew I wasn't happy. And now she knew my wife was a psycho.

I quietly opened the window and climbed out, just as Janay sent me a message back. I closed the window once I was all the way outside, and then went to respond to shorty's message.

Boom!

I fell to the ground, feeling something or someone on top of me, beating the fuck out of my back. I turned around and just as I'd figured, Lena's ass was going ham, slapping me in the back as if I didn't already have this fucking black eye.

"You...were...probably...going...to...see...that...hoe!" Lena hit me harder with each word she said, and she was becoming breathless, so her words came out slowly and deeply.

After taking a few more blows to the back from her manly ass hands, I just collapsed on our grass and let her finish giving me whatever punishment she felt like I deserved, right there in the broad daylight, with all of our neighbors laughing. Worst of all, Jayden and Kayden were on the porch pointing and laughing, watching their mom diminish whatever was left of my self-esteem.

The next day...
Janay told me that she worked at Kroger, so the way I got to see her was getting permission from Lena go to grocery shopping. Because she was insecure and controlling

as hell, she checked the mileage on the car before I left, and I knew she'd check it once I got back to make sure I only went there and back.

But, I wasn't worried about that right now. I wanted to see Janay. When my eyes landed on shorty, I felt a natural high overtake my body. Usually, I needed drugs and shit to make me feel like this, but just watching her do her thing at work was doing it for me today.

"What are you doing here? Will your wife be showing up to curse me out, again?" Janay asked sarcastically, as she left her register to talk to me. She threw up one of those "closed" signs and followed me to the Starbucks that was inside of the grocery store, and we sat down.

"I wanted to apologize for that shit, shorty. My fucking wife man...that bitch is different."

"Maybe she acts like that because she takes her vows seriously. I mean, most women do, I'm sure."

"You don't even know the half." I laughed, then explained to her how Lena cheated on me after getting fed up with my bullshit. The thing is, before Janay, I wasn't on that cheating shit anymore. Of course I looked, I lusted, I flirted...I was a fucking man. But since the first time I cheated on her, I hadn't actually fucked anybody else or been interested in anyone else. Until now.

"Wow. It sounds like you've got it pretty bad at home. Worse than I thought." Janay caught a tear that slipped from my eye, which was fucking crazy to me because I'd never in my life cried in front of a bitch before. Not even my own wife, and she did enough shit to me on the daily to make me want to cry. "I'm sorry, Weezy. I hope things get better for you."

"I don't. 'Cuz if things change at home, I wouldn't be able to get to know you."

I made her blush, but a nigga was speaking straight facts. I used to wish things would change for the better at home, just so I could have some type of peace of mind. But when I realized the shit wasn't happening, I started using drugs to cope with everything. I don't know if it was me just maturing or what, but I wanted real happiness. Not the kind drugs had to give me. It wasn't 'til recently that I realized I would never truly be happy with Lena, so I knew it was best to explore other options.

"Do you think you're going to file for a divorce?"

"I already tried." That was a few months ago, and all Lena did was give me a black fucking eye the day she got served with her papers. She told me I was never leaving her, but I could die trying. After that, I just left that shit alone. That's when I started developing my "I don't' give a fuck" attitude. That's exactly why I didn't give a fuck if she were to walk up behind me right now, flirting with the prettiest bitch I'd ever seen.

"Oh shit!" Janay shrieked, backing up from the table.

Once I felt a manly-ass hand yank back a handful of my dreads, I already knew what time it was. I guess I spoke too soon, because Lena was right here, whispering obscenities and threats to me.

"Get your short, lanky, ugly ass on, Weezy! Fuck you and everything you stand for! Cheating on me with the help from Kroger!"

She pulled me up by my ear, and dragged me out the side door, once again, giving a show to onlookers, and killing my self-esteem. I wish I could find it in my heart to put my hands on her the way she put her hands on me, but I can't.

Chapter Ten

DOMINO BLACK

A few days later...

I pulled up at The Black Palace, ready to see what the fuck Tatianna was so excited to show me. She'd been blowing my damn phone up, asking me to get here to see the surprise she had. I hoped it wasn't nothing stupid, because I hated when motherfuckers wasted my time.

When I walked inside, all the strippers were lined up, taking orders from Tatianna. I had to admit, they respected her a lot more than they respected Sherita. I think it's because she told them about her past as a stripper, and some of the bitches admired her and wanted to be in her position one day. Not at my club, though. I wouldn't hire none of these dusty foot bird bitches to do anything except shake their asses. Some bitches were only good for shit like that.

"So, what do you think, boss?" Tatianna walked toward

me, pointing her fingers at the girls, who were standing there skinning and grinning like I wanted their asses.

"About the fuck what?" I was confused and wasn't about to play her guessing games. I had shit to do.

Laughing, Tatianna brushed my arm with hand. She was getting way too comfortable already, which I didn't appreciate.

"Don't touch me." I moved her hand off my arm and repeated my question. "What do I think about what, Tatianna? I ain't gon' be here all day ake-ke-keing with your ass."

"The girls! I got some new girls, and all of them have on the uniforms I showed you."

Scanning the girls' bodies, I noticed they all had on the same type of lil' bras and thongs. Some had yellow sets, some had blue sets, and some had pink sets. They looked good, but not on everybody. That's why I told Tatianna I didn't want them in no fucking uniforms.

"I thought I told you no to the uniforms? You hard of hearing?"

"No." Tatianna chuckled, but there wasn't a damn thing funny. "I just thought – "

"I don't pay you to think. I pay you to do. Do what the fuck I say, and that includes getting rid of these uniforms."

I'd been in the strip club business for a while, and I knew for a fact that if a dancer wasn't one hundred percent comfortable in her attire, she wouldn't perform well. With that being said, some of these bitches liked the new uniforms, and others liked their old ones better. Some girls preferred to come out on the stage fully naked, and since they were dancing at a damn strip club, they had that right. Why make them cover up, even if it was just a little bit?

Tatianna nodded her head and instructed the girls to take off the uniforms. "I'll let the company know we're no longer going to use these, then. Are you at least happy with the new girls I've hired? Are you proud of me?"

Proud of her? I wasn't about to bow down and thank her for shit 'cuz at the end of the day, she was doing nothing but what the fuck I paid her to do. Motherfuckers always wanted rewards for doing their jobs. Plus, these new bitches she brought in here weren't the cutest at all. I walked down the line, staring all of 'em in their faces. There was one chick who stuck out her hand, but I slapped it back. "Don't touch me. How old are you?"

"Twenty-one." She replied, grinning in my damn face.

"Why do you look fifty? Get the fuck out of here. You're too smoked out for me."

I knew a crackhead when I saw one, and that bitch was definitely on some other shit. I couldn't have no females that weren't A1 working in my shit. One raggedy bitch could ruin it for everybody, and I didn't fuck with my money. Her face looked like a fucking rotten onion. The shit made me almost want to cry.

After the smoked out bitch left, I told Tatianna the others were fine.

"Alright ladies, back to the dressing room. Take off the

new outfits, and get back to practicing. We'll have a packed house tonight, and I need y'all dropping it and shaking it like your lives depend on it." Tatianna dismissed the girls but there was one who decided to stick around.

"What's your deal? Why the fuck you staring at me like you know me?" I asked, taking in her pretty complexion. She was one of those cute yet chubby girls; not my type, but I knew a few niggas who'd hit.

Instead of responding immediately, she just stood there nervously laughing. She finally spoke up after a few more seconds. "I'm Sunshine. I used to dance at The Gentleman's Corner. Remember?" She did a lil' twirl for me and although I didn't remember much about her, I did recall that I'd seen her face before. I hadn't seen her pussy in the air in a while, though, so I'd forgotten about her a long time ago.

Staring down at her body, I frowned. "Why are you built like a Teletubby? When was the last time you danced? You ain't in shape at all."

Shorty scowled, like I was trying to be rude to her. I wasn't rude. I was honest. And anybody working for me, representing my brand, The Black Palace, had to look the part. Ain't no way around it.

"Well, I just had a baby, so you could have some sympathy for my size. I'll go back down. My bounce back is real."

"Real slow, must be. How old is your baby? If he or she ain't two days old, your bounce back ain't shit. And I swear to God if you're popping your pussy and end up giving niggas a Bloody Mary show, I'm gonna blow your brains out myself."

Just the thought of that shit made me sick. These young bitches were funny as hell. So ready to dance on a pole, but not willing to take time off to raise their goddamn kids. That's the main reason why I was gon' have to kill whatever that was growing in Tierra's stomach before shit got out of hand. The only female I'd ever let have my baby was Bailee, and that's because she knew how to set priorities. These other bitches, like Tierra and obviously Sunshine, had their priorities fucked all the way up.

"Well, I would get to be home healing with my baby, if your brother took full responsibility of his seed."

My brother? Did I just hear her correctly?

Sunshine was standing with her arms folded across her chest, and when I gave her a quizzical look, she just nodded and smiled. "Yep. That's right. My daughter, Camia, belongs to your brother, Davion. And if he doesn't start being the family man he's supposed to be, he can kiss that little football career goodbye, because I'm coming for everything he has."

I yanked her by her throat, making her cough uncontrollably as I lifted her body in the air. Yeah, she was on the bigger side, but she damn sure wasn't bigger than me. I'd fuck this bitch up in a heartbeat if I wanted to. That wasn't my plan, though. I just wanted to scare her, so she would know I wasn't about to let her go through with her threats to ruin my brother's career. Lord knows he was doing a good enough job doing that on his own – that nigga needed all the help he could get, and I'll be damned if I let her fuck up the straight and narrow path I was trying to get and keep him on.

"If you even so much daydream about meddling in Davion's life, I'll end yours. You understand me, bitch?"

Gasping, she nodded her head. I shook her hard one time, and then put her back down on the floor.

"I didn't mean to start trouble, Domino. I just wanted to get the message to him that if he didn't do right by Camia, I would seek legal action."

"Bitch, you probably can't even afford legal action. I'm gonna let you work here until I see a paternity test that proves that your bald-headed baby is my brother's. If I don't get that within the next few weeks, you can consider yourself fired and dead to the entire Black family. And you may wanna figure out a day job 'cuz stripping ain't gon' work for you no more, looking like a fucking Zebra Cake." That bitch had me fucked up. True, Baby D was nothing but a dumb ass, I didn't allow no bitch to come up in here trying to violate me or my family. She was tripping hard.

"I'm just trying to make him pay for his actions, Domino!"

"I'm just trying to let you work so you can pay for a tummy tuck, Sunshine. Get yo' fat ass in the dressing room and take that ugly ass costume off before I knock you upside your lopsided ass head."

After her stupid ass got back on the stage, I sent a text to Davion to hit me ASAP. That lil' nigga had been a wild card lately, and now knowing he might not have one but two kids was crazy to me. The lil' fourteen-year-old he supposedly knocked up was still carrying her seed, but who knows when the lil' motherfucker was due? I knew for a fact that my brother couldn't handle not one or two kids — shit, the nigga can't even take care of himself. I had to find a way to get Sunshine out of his life before she ruined any chances he had left to go pro.

Two days later...
I'd gotten a call from Daria, my realtor, the day before yesterday, letting me know the Miami spot was basically mine. I just had to give some of the documents my John Hancock, and we were good to go. Daria said I could've done that shit via email, but I wanted to make sure every "I" was dotted and every "t" was crossed. As you already know, I was a businessman before anything, and my pops taught me at a young age to never assume shit. Always check shit out for yourself and make sure you know what you're getting into. So, that's why I was currently on the American Airlines plane headed to Miami for the night.

"I'm so excited for you. Miami is the first of many new clubs; I can feel it." Tatianna rubbed my kneecap and the only reason I didn't move it is 'cuz she was settling a little bit of the nerves I'd built up. But, if she moved her hand any further up my leg, I was gon' have to break her hand like I broke Tierra's foot. That was Bailee's property.

I know you're probably wondering why she was on the plane with me instead of my girl, but the answer was simple. Tatianna was a part of the business, and Bailee wasn't. Plus, Bai just started those cosmetology classes, and I didn't want her taking time off from school just to accompany me on a trip. She could save the few days she had to use for times when she'd really need them, like if she got sick or some shit. It just made more logical sense for Tatianna to go.

When we landed a couple of hours later, there was a limo there to pick us up from the airport. Tatianna had called some friend she had in town and ensured that we had the limo driver during our stay here, just so I didn't have to spend no money renting cars.

I gave the limo driver the address to the spot, and hit up Daria to let her know we were on the way. Bai had texted me twice while I was on the plane, so I was finally getting around to texting her back. She wanted to make sure I made it safely, and she told me to call her later. That I probably wouldn't be doing, since she wasn't aware that Tatianna was with me.

It's not like that between us, but I chose not to tell my girl because I knew how jealous she could be. I wasn't planning to do shit with Tatianna, so there was no need to worry her over nothing.

After responding to my girl's texts, and asking her for a video of her masturbating when she got a chance, I checked emails and by the time I looked up from my phone, we were pulling up to the spot.

"This is niceeee." Tatianna excitedly climbed out of the limo and admired the building that I too, was pretty proud of.

Daria introduced herself to Tatianna, and then we walked in to get a final walk through before signing on the dotted line.

. . .

*L*ater that night...

"You...are...the...bomb!" Tatianna lifted up her glass, clinking it with mine to toast to The Black Palace Miami. Everything was now official, and as soon as I found some girls to dance, I could set the opening date.

We were eating at the Otentic Fresh Food Restaurant on South Beach, celebrating, and while I was only slightly tipsy, Tatianna was so drunk she was liable to pass out at any moment.

"You're the best boss, ever. I wouldn't want to work anywhere else, or do anybody...I mean, do *business* with anybody else."

"Well, you make my job a little easier, and I thank you for all your hard work." I threw back the rest of my scotch as the waitress brought us both another round of drinks and shots.

"You know, I never asked you, but what hotel are we staying in? And what time are we leaving tomorrow?"

"Ten," I replied, throwing back the shot of Amsterdam that was on the table. "And we're staying at um...shit, I forgot. That motherfucker knows." I pointed to the limo driver, who was parallel parked outside of the restaurant, waiting on us. My buzz was starting to get to me, and I wasn't in the mood to do too much thinking. I just wanted to take my ass in my room and lay the fuck down.

After what seemed like hours but was only probably minutes, the waitress brought the check and I paid, then helped Tatianna out the door. She was stumbling and shit in her Giuseppe heels, but I caught her each time, making sure she didn't bust her ass.

Bailee had been blowing my damn phone up, and as I slid into the limo behind Tatianna, I was receiving my twenty-sixth call from her for the night. The problem was, I was planning to press ignore on this one, just as I'd done the others. I knew I was wrong for ignoring my girl, but a nigga was feeling good tonight and didn't want to be questioned or explaining myself. I just wanted to celebrate my success.

"Cheers!" Tatianna must've been reading my mind about wanting to celebrate, because she popped open the bottle of champagne that was in the back of the limo. Champagne splattered everywhere, leaving somebody a sticky mess to clean up. Not me, though. I was gon' take my ass up to this room and go to bed so I could get home to my girl tomorrow.

We pulled up to the hotel and when we got out, I grabbed both of our bags and checked in.

"I'm sorry, Mr. Black. We only have one room reserved for you. The other was given away accidentally, but we can upgrade the room you have to a suite if you'd like. You two would really enjoy it. Ocean view, a king-sized canopy bed, along with a full-sized – "

"We don't need all that shit. Just give me the key." I took the key from her and Tatianna and I rode to the third floor, where our room was.

"Bailee isn't going to have a problem with us sharing a room, is she?" Tatianna asked, after sitting down on the bed.

"I'm a grown motherfucker. Bailee and nobody else on this motherfucking earth runs me. You can have the bed, I'll take the couch."

I felt her eyes on me as I removed my shirt and my pants. "Goodnight," I said, as I turned off the lamp closest to the couch. I wasn't even in the mood to turn this motherfucker back and pull it out into the bed it had the ability to transform to. I was tired.

I woke up out of my sleep to a pair of lips wrapped around my dick. It felt good, but I knew it was wrong, since the lips didn't belong to my girl.

Tatianna was enjoying giving it to me as much as I was enjoying receiving head from her. I could tell by the way she moaned, slobbered, and jerked my shit as she bobbed her head. Fitting my entire pole in her mouth, she gagged on my shit as it scraped the back of her throat.

Nut came leaking out and Tatianna sucked up every bit. Wiping the corners of her mouth, she grinned and reached for my hand. "Let me make love to you, Domino. Let me show you what I've learned since the last time."

I pushed her off me and stood up to go wipe my dick off. "Sucking my dick was enough, Tatianna. You caught a nigga off guard but you know I got a fucking girl. Play your role and get in the fucking bed, and take your ass to sleep. Touch me again and I'll hang you by them long ass titties."

She climbed her thirsty ass back in the bed with a smirk on her face, but I was mad as shit. Mad that her dick sucking skills felt good – hell, even better than Bai's, but she'd never get the satisfaction of knowing that. I hated that I liked it and that I didn't stop her when I felt her lips on me, because I felt like I'd cheated on my girl. What really scared the fuck out of a nigga was that when I pulled up my pants, I felt my phone in my pocket, and when I grabbed it I saw Bailee's number on my screen, and she'd been on my call for over five minutes...

Chapter Eleven

TATIANNA

I don't know why he loves her. I honestly don't care, either. My motive isn't to get Domino Black to wife me. Hell, it's not even to get him to want to be with me. I applied for the job as his manager for one reason, and one reason only. And that's to help my man continue to build his empire. And no, I'm not talking about Domino.

My boyfriend – well sugar daddy, if you will – is James Montclair, one of South Carolina's most successful business-men. James takes good care of me, lacing with me with nothing but the most expensive diamonds, pearls, bags, and shoes. James is married, so he put me up in a penthouse in Columbia's wealthiest community, and anytime he's in town, he stays with me. Exotic vacations, a new whip every few months...all of these are just some of the benefits I get from being his girl. So when he asked me to help him take over

Domino's empire, I was left no choice but to help. After all, the money was going to benefit me in the end, anyway.

Many, many years ago, Domino's dad and James went into business together, or at least they were supposed to. Domino's dad didn't have all the funding he needed to get his store up and running, so James loaned it to him. Notice I said *loaned*. The business didn't last too long, but from my understanding, Domino's dad never paid James back. It was probably a good thing that he died when he did, because although James had enough wealth to last three lifetimes, he didn't play about his funds. If you owed him ten dollars, he expected that back, plus interest.

I said all of that to say that the reason James was going so hard to get a hand in The Black Palace was because he wanted to be paid back, and if Domino's dad couldn't do it, Domino would have to pay that debt. I was all for it, because he promised me a large portion of the profits.

My job was to come in as Domino's manager, and ensure that James' businesses profited from as much as possible. How was I going to do this? Well, the uniforms I'd ordered for the girls were my first attempt. James had a hand in a local designing company where we had the costumes made. But, Mr. Black wasn't quite feeling them. So, the next thing I was going to try to do was to make sure that James' liquor company was the sole provider of all the alcohol we served at The Black Palace. Before I was hired, James actually had a meeting with Domino, that didn't go too well, so it was up to me to persuade him. And I thought that by giving him some amazing head and pussy, that I could work on sealing the deal. But, all he wanted to do was be loyal to his girl...*after* I swallowed his cum. *Very loyal, Domino.*

Watching him twist and turn in this hotel room was hilarious to me, because the poor boy was clearly beating himself up over what he did to little miss Bailee. He was really going to be in for a rude awakening if he denied one more of my attempts to get James' businesses involved, because little did he know, I had a small recorder in my hand when I was giving him head. Yeah, he denied getting some of this gushy box, but he accepted my fellatio and was whimpering and whining like a baby. I could tell I'd sucked the soul out of him, and if Bailee was doing her job, she'd recognize his moans if she heard the recording. Seeing how much their little relationship meant to him, I'd hate to have to play it for her, just because he wouldn't agree to let my man have a hand in his business. Now if he agrees, Bailee will never have to know about his little episode of adultery and we can all live happily ever after. Win win situation for everyone.

Chapter Twelve

DAVION "BABY D" BLACK

The next morning...

Since my brother had gone out of town, he had no choice but to leave me in charge of The Black Palace last night, and you already know, I took full advantage of my position. Yes, I took some money from him, but this time it wasn't for a crazy reason. Shit, I really needed it. Not only did I need to get more coke, but I was also running low on my funds. Since Coach Starkes resigned, and he was the one who'd set up my stipend, I was no longer getting that. I also needed money for a lawyer, because this shit with Shanay was far from over.

I got a letter in the mail the other day from a law firm out of state, saying that once Shanay had her baby, they were summoning me to a paternity test, and if it came back that her lil' bastard baby was mine, I was gon' be put on child support. Not only that, but I'd have to register as a fucking sex offender, since the hoe was only fourteen and sixteen was the age of consent in our state. I'm hiring a lawyer to fight that shit, though, because I swear on my parents' graves I didn't know the damn girl was underage. Shit, there must be something in that motherfucking McDonald's or something, because when I was fourteen, the girls my age didn't look a damn thing like Shanay.

"We can prove that you were misled about her age, Mr. Black. But, I'll be quite honest with you. South Carolina laws are pretty strict about child molestation and rape. You may be sentenced and you may have to register as a sex offender for up to ten years. Do you have any kids?"

"Nah." In my eyes, I didn't. Camia still hadn't been proven to be mine, and I'd been staying my distance from her, just 'cuz her mama was having way too many fucking expectations, trying to be a family and shit.

"Good." The lawyer, Denise, a young, white chick with hair that was too goddamn long and needed to be cut, nodded her head and wrote some shit down on her legal pad. "Because the other suggestion I had is that while this is going on, you need to stay away from children."

"I can't stay away from kids, man. That shit is impossible. Do you know who the fuck I am? The season's starting next week and most of my fans are kids."

Denise threw her hands up and surrendered. "Fine. If you want to be around kids, by all means, do so. But don't be surprised if the blogs and news outlets eat that up, Davion. I'm just asking you to keep a low profile until we get in a court room and prove that you are innocent. If that's too much for you to do, then you can find another lawyer to represent you." She leaned back in her leather chair and tucked some of her dirty blonde hair behind her ear.

Her boldness surprised me, because everybody told Davion Black yes. But, I guess when you were making over eighty-five dollars an hour, you had the luxury of turning niggas down because you were gon' eat regardless. I didn't like that shit, though. Plus, I was desperate.

"What's my chances of getting into the pros at this point, Denise?"

"I'm a lawyer, not a sports analyst. But, given the fact that men in the NFL have similar and worse charges than what you're being accused for, I'd say that you still have a chance." She smirked, then continued. "The issue is, we want to make sure the NCAA doesn't kick you out, because if they do, you won't make it to the draft."

No shit, bitch.

The whole time she talked, I was thinking about two things – getting my next hit, and playing for the NFL. That shit was what I was born to do. Nobody, I mean nobody, could take away the joy I felt when I caught a football. The adrenaline that rushed through my body when I stepped on a football field was unmatched, and I literally felt like if I couldn't make a career out of playing the sport, there was no need for me to be alive.

. . .

𝒶 few hours later...
When I walked into my dorm, Domino was in the living area waiting on me. That fucking roommate of mine must've let him in, 'cuz he damn sure didn't have a Carolina Card to open that shit up.

"What you doing here?" I asked, wiping sweat off of my face with my Nike towel. After my meeting with Denise, I went to work out in the Strom Thurmond athletic center on campus, and I was just getting back to the room. I had football drills in about another hour, and after practice, I planned to either get my dick wet or get high. Whichever one I was able to do first, would be the activity I chose to partake in.

But here comes Domino, just messing up my entire vibe. Sitting on my couch with his arms folded across his chest and his jaws locked, he was giving off the impression that something was wrong. I just hoped if it was about the money I stole, he'd give me a chance to repay him before kicking my ass.

Without saying a word, Dom stood up and rushed over to me, lifting me up by the sweaty collar on my t-shirt. "Where the fuck is my money, Baby D? And not just the dough you took last night, either! All the shit you took before!"

His voice was so loud that I swore the walls vibrated. But, I wasn't about to show this nigga I was scared of him. If this nigga wanted smoke, I was gon' bring the grill.

"I ain't got no motherfucking money!"
Wham!

Domino slammed me on my back on the kitchen floor of my dorm. His huge body was on top of mine, and the look in his eyes told me he wasn't playing. I thought the nigga was about to kill me for a second. "Where is my fucking money?"

"I'll pay you back, Dom. I swear! I needed it...for a lawyer!"

I guess he felt sorry for me, because he extended his hand and helped me up. "Nigga, don't I take care of you? Aren't you my fucking brother? If you need something, ask, don't steal. I've killed niggas for less money than you've taken from me. If it happens again, I'm chopping your fucking hands off, and you'll never be able to steal or throw a football again."

I believed him.

"Are you coming to my first game next week?"

"Is my name Domino Black? I'll be there, motherfucker. I told you I'm proud of you. Just stop doing dumb shit. You gon' fuck around and make me kill yo' stupid ass." Without another word, he left out of my dorm and when I saw his car leave the parking lot, I knew the coast was clear. I smiled to myself as I pulled out the remaining funds I had from what I stole from him – I had a cool two stacks left after paying the lawyer. Shit, with that, I could buy enough rocks to last me for the next week. Thanks, Domino.

One week later...
     The Williams Brice Stadium was filled with USC Gamecock fans cheering and clapping for me. Yes, me.

The star quarterback. The first black quarterback in years. *The* Davion Black. It was down to the last two minutes of the fourth quarter, and we were tied with The University of Florida. The fucking Gators, our long-time rivals.

I received the ball from the center, and as soon as I got possession, I turned around and ran as fast as I could toward the line. Hearing all the fans cheer my name, telling me to go faster, gave me all the ammunition I needed to make it to the line and give us the touchdown that would win us the game.

Crack!

I felt myself fall, twisting my ankle in the most uncomfortable position it'd ever been in. Even if I had something to smoke, that shit wouldn't have taken away this pain.

Rolling on the grass, I heard the fans calling my name, yelling for me to get up, but I just couldn't. The medical crew rushed over and put me on a stretcher, and the only thing I could think about was my career ending on the day it truly began.

*T*en *minutes later...*

"It's not too bad, son. Your ankle is sprained. Really, really, badly. You might have to be out for a few months, but at least there should be no long-term damage."

I couldn't believe my fucking ears right now. I'd gone eighteen years without even so much as a minor cut, so to have a sprained ankle during what was supposed to be the start of my collegiate football career was devastating.

The doctor wrapped my ankle, and while he was doing that, the door opened and Dom and Dedrick rushed in.

"Are you okay, Davion? That looked like it hurt," Dedrick said, eyeing my foot.

No shit, Sherlock.

I didn't even waste my time responding to that dumb ass statement. "I have a sprained ankle, so I won't be out too long. This shit fucking sucks, though. I need all the playing time I can get."

"You've got to make sure you're healthy, and that your ankle heals. That's the most important thing." Camiyah walked in, holding the baby that I didn't even know was out of the hospital, and came to sit beside me. "You'll be okay. You were there for me when I got shot, and I'll be there for you now."

I wasn't there for her ass when she got shot. Not after the first day. And little did she know, the only reason I had done that much was because I knew the feds were gon' be all over that shit, and I needed to monitor what was said. I wasn't up there with her because I wanted to be.

"Well, it looks like you're covered, lil' bro. I got shit to do, so we're gon' roll out. You got him, Sunshine?"

I chuckled at Domino calling Camiyah by her old stage name. I didn't even think the nigga remembered or even knew her name. He was eyeing Camia, like he was trying to figure out if she was mine or not. I hadn't told him about her yet, but I guess the cat was out the bag now.

Camiyah nodded her head and kissed the top of Camia's.

"I got him. *We* got him."

My brothers walked out, and Camiyah planted a kiss on my cheek as the doctor brought me a wheelchair and placed me in it. Holding Camia up on her shoulder, she used her one free hand to roll me out of the door.

I couldn't lie, I did appreciate the fuck out of her for doing this, 'cuz as you can see, my brothers dipped quickly as fuck. I couldn't blame them, though. Me and Dedrick had never been tight like that, but my relationship with Dom had been so rocky lately that I didn't expect him to stay and help me. Would've been nice if he did, but I guess he was teaching me not to bite the hand that fed me.

"Thanks, Camiyah. You didn't have to do this."

She hit the wheelchair access button the wall so the door would open automatically for us. Rolling me out the door, she laughed. "I know I didn't. But, I want us to have a good relationship. For Camia's sake. After all, we're family."

The moment she said the word "family", Celine's eyes met with mine. They were full of hurt, although according to our last encounter when I went to see her, she was done with me. I guess she was coming back there to check on me, but in all honesty, fuck her. She was nothing but a hoe and she was engaged to be married anyway, to that corny nigga's son, so why the fuck would I waste my time fucking with her? I didn't have any fucks left to give, especially to a bitch who spoke broken English.

Staring Celine in her eyes, I smirked and replied to Camiyah. "You're right, baby. We're family."

Chapter Thirteen

BAILEE RODGERS

he next day...

Between school and helping my man get shit together for this Miami opening, I'd been so busy lately. Not that I was complaining, because cosmetology school was so fulfilling that I couldn't even explain it, but I needed a day of rest. I could almost feel my body breaking down on me, so when Dom woke me up this morning with breakfast in bed, some phenomenal oral sex, and a massage, I was extremely appreciative.

"What you getting into today?" He asked me, feeding me the last strawberry out of my homemade fruit bowl. Living with him was crazy, but in a good way. Spontaenous. Fun. I was literally doing life with my best friend, and gestures like this definitely kept the spark in our relationship.

"I just want a day to sleep, baby. I'm so tired."

Domino shook his head. "Well, that's not gonna happen. I got some shit set up for you, so your ass bet not fall asleep."

My curiosity got the best of me. I lifted my eyebrows and stared at my man's sexy chocolate face, searching for a hint. Finally, I asked, "Shit like what?"

"A real massage, since you and I both know I don't know what the fuck I'm doing. And an appointment at the nail salon. Them nubs you got...they're childish. I want you to dig in my back, not tickle it."

"Whatever, nigga!"

I hated that I had to take my fake nails off when I started cosmetology school, because they were getting in the way. I did miss my nails, so I was glad he suggested I get them done. I didn't even realize guys paid attention to shit like that. But then I had to remember who I was dealing with – Domino, the hygiene king. It was funny hearing the things he found attractive and unattractive.

After the two of us showered together, Domino left the house first. He said he had to get to The Black Palace for a meeting with Tatianna, and although I trusted my man, I couldn't help but wonder if he'd set this little day up for me so I wouldn't be around to interrupt the two of them.

Let's be clear. I wasn't jealous. I wasn't insecure. I was inquisitive. And the fact that Tatianna was around Domino almost as much as I was didn't calm my curiosity. On top of that, I couldn't deny that she was pretty. I trusted my man, but recent events had taught me that I couldn't trust bitches around my man, and that reason alone was why I was planning to do a little pop up at his club before I went to all these appointments he'd set for me.

Slipping on a white off the shoulder top and black biker shorts, I pulled my hair up into a high pony tail and slipped on my black and white vans. I'd straightened my hair the other day at school, and had been wearing it down my back since then. But, just in case I had to drag a bitch, I wanted it in a ponytail.

Pulling up at The Black Palace, I quickly threw my car in park and grabbed Domino's old wallet before getting out. See, I had the perfect plot. My man didn't like jealousy, so I planned to just "pop in" with his old wallet, pretending to forget that he'd recently gotten a new one. That gave me the excuse I needed to be here. Not that I needed one, because I was his lady, but I'd feel better about spying on him if I told him that little white lie.

Loud music pierced my ears as I walked inside, and watching the girls dance and gear up for tonight, I instantly got horny. Not that I was gay or anything, but the way these bitches were shaking their asses made me want to shake something for my man in his back office. Hopefully he was down for a quickie...

"I'm just wondering why you won't take my advice on this, Domino. You know I'm right. I know I'm right. It'll save you a ton of money and time. By the way...you look good in this shirt."

Yank!

I grabbed Tatianna by her long hair, making her fall on the ground.

"Ouch!" She screamed, as I slapped her in her face.

"Don't you ever put your hands on my man again, bitch! And if you even think about it, you'll regret it!"

Domino smirked, and told her to get out of his office. Once we were alone, he sat me on the desk, and stuck his tongue down my throat. "You were spying on me, baby?"

"No...you left your...your wallet at home."

"Don't lie to me, Bail." He pressed against me with his growing, throbbing, thick manhood. "You were spying on me? You think I'm trying to fuck with another bitch?"

"No." I shook my head, just as Dom grabbed my face with his strong hands.

"You know I gotta punish you for lying, right? You know good and goddamn well you didn't come up here to bring me a raggedy ass wallet. Open your legs."

I didn't even get a chance to spread them, because he did it for me. Domino stuck his strong hand down in my biker shorts, while using the other to fondle my breasts. Feeling my kitty beginning to purr, I laid back on his desk, giving him easier access to pull my shorts down, which he did with a quickness.

"Why the fuck you not wearing panties, Bai?" Domino asked, dipping his tongue in and out of my opening.

"I wanted to make it easy for you, daddy," I moaned, enjoying the way his tongue against my clit felt.

He must've been pleased with that answer, because he

buried his head deeper in my love tunnel, licking me harder and faster. As he ate me out, he continued to play with my nipples, causing my body to convulse from the amazing feeling of being stimulated in both areas at once. I creamed in his mouth, and once he lapped my juices up, he told me to bend over, which I did.

Pounding me from the back, he pulled my hair and gently choked me with each stroke.

"I...love...you...Dom!" I could hardly get my words out because he was beating it up so good. His dick was so deep inside of me that it felt like it was in my stomach. Domino was definitely blessed down below.

"I love yo' ass too, girl," he panted. Within seconds, we released our fluids simultaneously, leaving a sticky mess between both of our legs.

*O*ne *hour later...*
As I was getting my massage, I received a phone call from Celine, which I thought was odd, given the fact that we hadn't spoken in a few days. Things were really iffy between us because of all the back and forth between her and Davion, so I told myself I would wait for her to hit me up instead of reaching out. Not only that, but I wasn't sure if I could trust her since she was still living in the town house with Rhyan. Well, I think she was. Janay ended up not moving in since there was so much tension between all of us, so I hadn't been there to visit.

"Mamacita! Donde esta? Where are you? Let's go get lunch. I need to talk."

Hearing her voice made me miss her a bit, so I agreed to meet her after my massage. I had an hour to spare before my nail appointment, so we decided to meet at San Jose's. She loved eating Mexican food, and I loved their margaritas.

We pulled up at the restaurant at the same time, and she immediately ran over to give me a hug. "I have to tell you so much, chica! I missed you!"

"I've missed you too. Let's go inside."

After ordering our food and drinks, Celine got right to it. "I miss him, mami. I know I shouldn't, but I do. And I want him. I think. No se. I'm so confused!"

I didn't have to ask who she was talking about. Davion's ass. I decided to keep my opinions to myself, though. Dom told me that Davion supposedly had a baby with some stripper, and I'd rather not be the one to tell Celine the bad news.

"I saw him yesterday. I went to his game." She took a sip of her margarita as soon as the waitress brought it out. "I think he has a baby, chica! A little nina. Some girl was wheeling him out after he got hurt, and he told them they were a family. Can you believe it?"

Yes.

"You deserve better, Celine." That was all I could think of to say, without confirming or denying anything she just said. One thing I'd learned from being with Domino was that you couldn't help who you loved, but on the flip side, I also wanted to give her an honest opinion of mine. It was no secret that I wasn't fond of Davion, for more than one reason, and I personally felt that Celine could do a lot better.

"I could say the same about you, mami. Does Domino even treat you right?"

"Surprisingly, yes." I nodded, accepting my enchilada meal from the waitress. Most people would be surprised by the fact that Domino Black would treat a woman right, but I had no complaints. Of course he had a foul mouth and was violent to those that crossed him, but he treated me so much differently. The difference between me and Celine's situations were that I couldn't say that about Davion.

"I'm sorry, chica. That was rude. I guess I'm just confused. Like, how can Domino be the perfect man, but Davion isn't?"

"Domino's not perfect, Celine. Nobody is. Trust me, bitches are always in my man's face and even on his phone. But he knows what he's got at home. The difference between him and Davion is that Davion doesn't value you. He doesn't know what it's like to miss you. When Dom and I first met, I made it known that I would leave his ass if he ever tried to play me. Men like standards. They act like they don't, but if you just let 'em do you any kind of way, then that's what the fuck they're going to do."

I wasn't trying to preach at my girl, but I was stating nothing but facts. Celine had sat there and accepted Davion back with open arms each time he fucked up, so he'd probably gotten used to taken advantage of her. The problem with that was that the one time a bitch said "no", all hell would break loose. Davion was spoiled and in my opinion, not deserving of a girlfriend until he got out of all this legal trouble and grew the fuck up.

Nodding her head, Celine seemed to take in all the gems I was dropping on her regarding Baby D. I could only pray that she understood where I was coming from, and made him work for her, instead of continuing to throw herself at him. That shit was pitiful.

A *few days later...*
My man had convinced me to get social media accounts, since at school, we'd soon be taking appointments and getting paid a small percentage of the fees the clients were charged. So, that's what I was currently doing – creating my page. I had no idea how to work Snapchat, so I created an Instagram handle and began uploading pictures from my phone of hair I'd done both in my spare time and on the mannequins at school.

As I was going through my phone, I accidentally ignored my dad's call, sending him to voicemail. When I went to check the message he left, I saw that I had one deleted voicemail, so I decided to check it. I didn't recall deleting any messages, and was hoping it was nothing or nobody important. When I saw it was from Domino's number, I decided to listen to it, just in case it was something important.

My jaw dropped all the way down to the floor when the message began playing. The sounds of moaning and slurping filled my ear, as tears filled my eyes. I knew that moan anywhere. It was definitely Domino, and he was getting some head. I knew how he sounded when my wet mouth hit his penis, and it was extremely similar to the sounds coming through my phone.

Checking the date on the message, I saw where it matched the date he went to Miami to seal the deal on The Black Palace Miami. So many thoughts ran through my head, but instead of going off, I decided to pack all my shit up and leave. I just had a talk with Celine the other day about not accepting bullshit from Davion, and here I was, in the same situation with his brother.

Once I had all my shit packed up in suitcases, I grabbed the keys to the Benz he bought me not too long ago and began putting all my bags in the car. He wasn't home, but his Maserati was, since he was driving his other car today. So, I decided to leave him a little gift.

Boom! Boom!

I kicked his car so fucking hard that the sides of it became dented. Then, I took a pin out of my hair and used it to flatten two of his tires. The only reason I didn't pull a Jazmine Sullivan and go crazy busting the windows was because I was too emotionally drained to finish the job. I wanted to lay down. I wanted to cry. I wanted to forget Domino Black ever existed. I put his number on the block list and decided that I would start fresh; fuck him.

. . .

*O*ne *hour later...*

I hadn't been at my parents' house for a full hour yet, and my mom was already irking my nerves. I didn't say anything about why I was back here with all my stuff, but of course she assumed the worse — that Domino had broken my heart. It killed me that she was right, but I didn't give her the satisfaction of knowing that. I made it seem like I just came to visit and switch out some of the things in my closet, but I could tell she knew I was lying.

Janay sent me a text, asking if I could accompany her tonight to another party. The last party ended up being for Domino's friend, and the last thing I wanted to do was run into his ass tonight. I was on pins and needles praying he didn't come over here once he realized me and all my stuff was gone.

I replied back to Janay, denying her, but then she hit my texts with this sob story about this being the last time and her really needing me. I finally agreed, and she said she'd be by to pick me up in an hour, so I went ahead and got dressed for the night.

Once she arrived, I was just finishing up my makeup.

"Damn, Bailee. You look cute! You might steal my job for the night." Janay joked, watching me put the finishing touches on my outfit.

I was wearing a black sleeveless dress that was sheer in the middle and showed all the parts of my body that the good Lord took his time making. My long black hair was straightened with a middle part, and it fell down the middle of my back. I wasn't big on makeup, but tonight, my face was beat. I did a smoky-eye look, and added some foundation and bright red lipstick to match my nails and toes.

"You do too," I complimented Janay, who was wearing a white bandeaux top and a tight, white short skirt. Since it was August in South Carolina, it was hot as fuck, so a few of her curls had fallen. I re-curled her hair, and we were soon out the door.

We pulled up to a house that was damn near a mansion, and there were people everywhere. What made me uncomfortable was that most of them were niggas.

"Where are we?" I asked, as soon as she parallel parked her car on the side of the house.

Excitedly, Janay squeezed my arm. "Tony Marshall's listening party! I got asked to dance here, can you believe it?"

Who dances at a listening party? "*The* Tony Marshall?"

"Yes, girl! I can't believe it!"

Tony Marshall was one of the most famous R&B singers today. He had hits such as "Love You Better", "Making a Baby With You", "Die in Your Arms", and many more songs that would make you want to hump your man in front of his mama if she was in your way. He happened to be a hometown legend since he was from Columbia; even though he didn't live here anymore, I could vouch for the fact that he always showed the city love when he had the opportunity. He wasn't one of those celebs who forgot where they were coming from.

I just had one question for Janay. "How did you land this gig?"

"The power of social media girl," she replied giggling. I wasn't mad at her. I'd just made my Instagram account today, and had already booked two appointments for next week, so I was proof that social media was definitely a great networking tool. But to book a gig for Tony Marshall? That was crazy!

When we got to the front door, we were greeted by a security guard, who must have liked what he saw since his eyes wouldn't stop roaming our frames. When he put his hands on us to see if we had weapons, he moved his hands slowly around our curves, and I felt violated as fuck. The only reason I didn't show out was because I knew this was a big deal for Janay. Otherwise, he would've gotten a taste of the pepper spray that was in my purse.

I didn't know whether this was Tony Marshall's house or not, but once we got in, I was in awe. The outside didn't do this place any justice. The foyer was the size of a small ballroom, and was decorated like one as well. The chandeliers hanging from the ceiling were pretty as hell, and all the plaques on the walls gave this place flavor, too.

"You ladies like what you see?"

We turned around at the same time to find Tony Marshall smiling at us, holding a drink in his hand. Janay was the first to speak. "I'm Janay. Your assistant hired me to do some dancing. This is my friend, Bailee."

"Bailee." Tony Marshall licked his lips, extending his hand to me. "I'm Tony."

"I know," I blushed. "Who doesn't know you?"

"You're right." He threw back the rest of his drink and told us to follow him.

We got to a room that I assumed was a guest bedroom, and he told us to change, so of course, I had to correct him.

"I'm not a stripper. I'm just here with my friend." I explained, shaking my head when he told us to get dressed.

Grabbing me by my waist, he smiled as his hands rubbed the small of my back. "Well, you can come with me then." I was feeling slightly uncomfortable, so I inched away from him, but he kept his hands on my waist.

I told Janay to text me if she felt uneasy, but she told me she'd be fine. "Where is everybody? There are an ass of cars outside." I commented, following Tony Marshall down a long hallway.

"Downstairs."

He led me to the basement, which was as big as my parents' den, kitchen, and backyard combined. The crowd of people was so thick that I could hardly move from one end of the room to the next. I saw a lot of celebrities in there, which was crazy because there was nothing on the radio or on TV advertising this party. But, it was packed as hell. Tony Marshall left me to go grab the microphone from the deejay.

"Alright, alright. We got some entertainment coming through, then when that's over, we're gon' listen to my new album, alright? Y'all motherfuckers are getting the first listen, so let me hear you make some noise!"

The crowd, including me, went crazy. Within a few

seconds, I saw Janay making her way down the stairs in nothing. Literally, nothing. Men, who were the majority tonight, whistled and tried to touch her as she walked past them, heading for the middle of the floor. I was so uncomfortable for her, but she didn't seem to have one care in the world. I knew she'd do almost anything for her money, but damn.

Tony Marshall had a stripper pole in the middle of the floor, which was where Janay immediately ventured to. Watching her dance was almost painful, because I was hearing all the comments being made about her. None of them were bad, but most of them were disrespectful to her as a woman, and that bothered me, since she was my friend.

As she shook her ass to Ginuwine's "Pony", I felt a pair of hands caress my ass. Turning around, I saw that it was Tony Marshall.

"You know you're fine as fuck, Bailee. I wouldn't mind showing you a thing or two upstairs in my room."

Excuse me?

"I'm good. I just came to...to support my girl."

Pow! Pow! Pow!

The sounds of gunshots interrupted the party, as everyone began to run for cover. Tony Marshall and a couple of other niggas, who I assumed were a part of his posse, took out guns, but everyone else tried to flee.

The lights were off in the basement, so when a tall dark figure walked in with a gun in the air, I damn near peed on myself. This felt just like a horror movie, and I just knew I was about to lose my life.

"Bring yo' motherfucking ass on, Bailee!"

Before I could respond, I was lifted in the air and tossed over a shoulder. A strong, sturdy shoulder that smelled just like Dior cologne. "How did you know I was here, Domino? Put me down! And where is Janay?"

"I don't know where the fuck that hoe is, and I really don't care. She ain't my concern; you are. You're coming with me. Fuck is your problem?"

What is *my* problem? How could he ask me that? He was so stupid!

"*You* are my problem, Domino!" When we got to the front door, I saw that he'd killed the security guard, because he was lying at the door in a pool of his own blood.

As if reading my mind, Domino shrugged his shoulders nonchalantly, as if he didn't drop a body in cold blood. "The nigga wasn't trying to let me in."

I followed him to his car, crying and yelling at the same time. "You didn't have to *kill* him, Domino!"

"And instead, what? Risk you getting killed or hurt or raped or some shit?"

"Why would it matter? When I was raped, you were nowhere to be found! You were too busy fucking around with Sapphire!"

I really didn't mean for that to slip out, but I think I'd been holding it in for so long that it was bound to spill from my lips one day. Tears filled my eyes as I watched Domino stare at me in disbelief. Nausea began to settle in, as I relived the night Tyler violated me in my own parents' home.

"What the fuck did you just say, Bailee?"

Nodding my head, I twirled a strand of my hair, which was something I did when I was nervous and not wanting to face the truth. "It's true," I whispered. "The night you broke into my house, remember? Before you got there, Tyler came in and raped me because he was angry I'd moved on."

"Man, fuck!" Domino hit his hand on the steering wheel so hard I thought he was going to break it. "Where the fuck is that nigga at, Bai? Where the fuck can I find him?"

"I don't know!"

I just wanted to forget about the whole thing, but I knew Domino well enough to know that he would want to settle the score with Tyler.

Domino snatched my phone out of my hand and entered the code in, then gave me my phone back. "Call that nigga. Right now. Tell him you wanna see him. And take me to his crib. Now!"

I did as requested, and within fifteen minutes, we were pulling into Tyler's yard.

"Stay here." He kissed me passionately, like he thought it could've been our last one, and then he got out the car.

Tyler opened the front door, but as soon as he realized the person coming to the porch was Domino and not me, he tried to slam it shut. But, it was too late. Domino tackled him like the football player he used to be in high school, causing him to fall on the porch. Domino jacked Tyler up and threw him on the hood of his car, then backed up about one hundred feet. Tyler and his mom lived near the woods, so no one heard Tyler's pleas for help when Domino put his pistol to his head.

"Bailee. Get out the car and get a stick. A big one."

I handed Domino the stick, but he gave it back to me. "Stick him the ass, baby. Rape that nigga like he raped you."

Tyler yelped out in pain, as I shoved the stick up the crack of his ass. Since he'd answered the door with nothing but boxers on, I had the perfect entrance to his skinny ass hole.

"Ouchhhh! Fuckkkk!" Tyler yelled, feeling the stick go in and out of his butt.

I was getting such pleasure from seeing him struggle the same way he made me struggle. I had no sympathy for this man. I wanted to violate him just as he'd done me, and let him feel the agony and embarrassment I would forever have to live with as a result of what he did to me.

"Alright, that's enough." Domino took the stick from me and threw it on the ground. Cocking his gun, he then pointed it right at Tyler's head. "Any last words?"

Pow!

Even if Tyler did have last words, Dom didn't give enough time for him to say them. But, I didn't care. I know it sounds fucked up, but I was happy that he was dead. Maybe now he'd stop consuming my thoughts, because I would often have nightmares about what he'd done to me.

"Get in the car."

I did as my man instructed me to, and after he made a quick phone call, he got in the car and we drove off, leaving Tyler's body on the ground. I guaranteed it wouldn't be there for long, though. Domino told me a while back that he had some guys who disposed of bodies he killed for him. I didn't ask any other details, simply because some things I'd rather not know.

Some things I did need to know, though.

"Baby. How did you know where I was?"

"I know everything. And one thing I damn sure know is that you better be moving your shit back in the house tonight. And denting my car ain't gon' do shit, baby girl. I don't give a fuck about that car."

I laughed, because I really thought I was hurting him by messing with his car. He was sadly mistaken if he thought he was winning me over though, because I wasn't doing shit. Not without the explanation I was waiting on, first. There was a reason I moved out in the first place. "Domino, I'm not moving back in with you. You let a bitch suck you up in Miami, didn't you?"

"Nah. I didn't let anybody do shit."

"Liar!" I clocked him upside the head, hitting him hard as hell. Then, I scratched him with my nails so deep that he started bleeding. *Yeah, you wanted me to get my claws back, right?*

"What the fuck, bi – "

"Call me a bitch and I'll pepper spray you!"

By now, he'd pulled over on the side of the road to nurse his little cut. Domino should've known better than to fuck with me. I was just as crazy as he was.

"I'm not one of those weak bitches like Tierra, Domino. Do not try to run game on me. Who was giving you head in

Miami and why? So it's cool if I let another nigga slide his tongue all up and through my box?"

"Watch your motherfucking mouth." Domino spat, as he got a napkin from his glove compartment and wiped the spot where he was bleeding. "I love you, baby. You fucking know that shit, too. Don't you?"

"I thought I did. But after hearing the voicemail you left me...I'm not so sure." A lone tear slid down my face, and Domino wiped it.

"I can't stand to see you cry, Bailee. Especially not over some shit that I did. You want the truth?"

Duh, nigga. What else would I want, a lie?

"Here's the truth." Domino lifted my chin with his hand kissed me before continuing. "I didn't go to Miami alone. I took Tatianna, only because she's the manager."

Before he finished his statement, I'd slapped the taste out of his mouth. I couldn't believe he'd gone out of town with that bitch! I slapped him one more time and yanked on his door, trying to get out of the car.

"Bailee! What the fuck, girl! A nigga's trying to tell you the truth and shit, and here you are, tripping! That's why I didn't wanna tell your ass in the first place. It ain't even like that, but you wanna bitch and shit!"

That hurt, because I told myself I would always want to be the type of girlfriend who could take the truth, no matter how ugly it was. *Check yourself, Bailee.* "Fine." I crossed my arms along my chest and sighed deeply. "Continue." I still was heated, though. The nerve of him...

"The bitch came with me, just 'cuz she works with me, alright? The fucking hotel staff messed up our shit, giving us one room instead of two. I took the couch; I let her get the bed. I was knocked the fuck out, and when I woke up, she was sucking me off. I pushed her off me, swear to God." He did the cross over his chest to let me know he was serious, but I was still pissed. I was just about sick of Tatianna and her little antics. It was evident that she wanted my man, and if he wasn't going to put her in her place, I was.

"Don't worry. I put that bitch right in her place. And I put that on my parents' grave, Bai," Domino promised, staring at me with those sexy ass eyes. He made it so hard to be mad at him. "I love you, alright? I'm not letting that bitch break us apart, and neither should you." He pulled me into his strong arms and stroked my back gently.

"Fire her. Immediately. Because I'm liable to choke the bitch."

Dom laughed, but I wasn't a fucking clown. Realizing I was serious, he gave me kiss on the lips. "That hoe knows her place, alright? But if she steps to me one more time, I'm giving you the okay to beat her ass. Shit, I'll record that motherfucker and throw it on World Star if you want me to."

Finally laughing, I leaned over and gave him a hug. "Thank you, Dom. For telling me the truth, saving me tonight, and for getting Tyler back. I guess I just...I'm scared to lose you to another girl."

"I ain't met a bitch yet with pussy as wet as yours, so you don't have shit to worry about."

Speaking of my pearl, she was throbbing for his touch. It's crazy how I could be so mad at him one minute, and turned on by him the next. After we'd just committed a damn murder.

Taking his hand in mine, I placed it on my drenched twat, and let him play inside of me until we got back to his house. Our house. I had plans of moving my things back in tomorrow morning, because there was nowhere I'd rather be than with him. Call me crazy if you want to, but Domino's story seemed sincere, and unless I found out otherwise, I didn't plan on losing him.

Chapter Fourteen

DEDRICK BLACK

The next evening...

*L*ife has been pretty darn – *damn* – good to me lately. My fall classes were going well so far, and Brittany helped me back to school shop a few days ago, and I've also been making friends. I mean, I always had friends, but they were nerds like me. These new friends were...popular. The cool guys. I no longer felt like an outcast at USC, and I had Brittany to thank for that. We didn't hang out much outside of school, but hopefully that would change soon. It was weird. I'd call and text her in the evenings, but sometimes, hours would go by without a response. I guess she was just busy. I admired her work ethic. *Hustle.* That's the cool word, right?

Right now, I was getting dressed so I could take her on another date. A real one, this time. Not the McDonald's drive-thru. And the best part about this date was that it was a surprise. I was going to drive to her house just to show her how much effort I was willing to put in. After all, she was my first...my last...and my only.

Looking in the mirror, I smiled when I saw my appearance. I was wearing a black Armani shirt, along with black Armani jeans and one of the gold chains Domino gave me around my neck. Even though I missed my suspenders and high-waisted khaki pants, I liked that I now looked like a snack. *Did guys look like snacks, or was that just for girls?* I looked so different, but I knew I appealed more to Brittany this way. So, it was fine by me.

I brushed my teeth once more before heading out, and after letting my car run for about seven minutes, I was able to drive off and head to Brittany's house. I couldn't wait to surprise her. I knew that it was always nice to romance your girl, so I wanted to make sure I was on top of my game. I stopped and got roses and a box of chocolates, just because I knew women appreciated the small things.

When I rang the doorbell, it took a few minutes for her to open the door. When she finally did, she didn't seem as happy as I'd hoped. "What are you doing here, Dedrick? I didn't know you were coming by. Is there a reason you're here?"

"A reason? To...to see you." I hoped that wasn't a problem. If we were courting, I didn't see why it would be. Being in her presence was all I wanted to do.

Wearing nothing but a silk robe, she stood in front of me looking like a goddess. My penis – *dick* – rose to the occasion, and I desperately wanted to take her in whichever room was hers, and do the same thing we always did when we saw each other. The nasty. The grown man.

Since the first time we had intercourse, we'd done it about three more times, and each time got better and better for me. I was really learning my way around a vagina.

That's the main reason I wanted to take Brittany on a date tonight. I wanted to show her that it wasn't just about sex. I wanted to show her that I was really digging her vibe. *Did I say that right?*

I'd never had the chance to show a female how sweet I could be, because I was never noticed by anyone. Now that I had a real girlfriend, I wanted to give my all.

"I wanted to take you on a date, Brittany." I explained, trying to push the door open to let myself in. She wouldn't let me though. I've never been inside of her house, and I was starting to wonder what she was hiding in there.

"It's not a good time, Dedrick. You have to...you have to let me know things in advance, okay? Like let me know when you're wanting to drop by here. I have shit to do. And it doesn't include you."

She slammed the door in my face, and although I tried to mask it, I was completely heartbroken.

One hour later...
Since Brittany didn't want to hang out with me tonight, I decided to call up my brother Domino, to see if I could hang out with him at The Black Palace. I'd only been

there once, and although the atmosphere was different than what I was used to, I did enjoy hanging out with my brother. It felt like I was getting time back from when we were growing up, since we never really clicked like that. Plus, I just wanted to be around some good energy. My heart was still aching from my encounter with Brittany earlier, and I wanted some laughs and a good time.

When I arrived, I had to call Domino to the front because the bouncer at the door didn't recognize me as his brother, and was trying to make me pay.

"Thanks," I said shyly, as Domino explained to him who I was. The bouncer let me in and apologized to Domino.

"My bad, man. I didn't know the lil' nerdy motherfucker had that much swag."

I guess I should take that as a compliment?

I could barely walk to the VIP area, because it was so packed in the club. Slow, seductive music that I'd never heard before played loudly as the girls climbed poles, danced on guys, and collected the money being thrown at them. When I finally sat down in the VIP area, I was greeted by Bailee, Weezy, and another girl. I looked around to see if Lena was anywhere in the vicinity, because Weezy and the girl were looking pretty cozy, but there were no signs of Lena there. Yet.

"I'm Janay." She extended her hand and then sat back on Weezy's lap, dancing in it slowly. Seeing both she and Weezy, along with Dom and Bailee coupled up made me miss Brittany.

"I gotta go." I stood up and walked out of the club, ready to go back to my girl. I didn't care that she said she had stuff to do. We could chill at her house if she wanted. I just wanted to be around her, no one else...

Before arriving at Brittany's house for the second time tonight, I stopped by Walmart to grab a bouquet of roses. Earlier today, it was just a bag with four roses in it, but tonight, I got a full blown bouquet. Maybe that will make her want me.

When I knocked on her door, she took forever to open it. "Dedrick? Why are you back here? Did you not understand you can't just pop up on me?"

"I wanted to give you these." I handed her the flowers, and her face softened. *Score!* "May I come in?"

"More flowers? That's a bit much...don't you think?" She rolled her eyes and sighed, then finally gave in to my wishes. "I'll be out in a second. Okay?"

Cheesing like a kid on Christmas, I nodded my head and went back to my car. Brittany came out a few minutes later, and it was really hard trying to read her expression when she got in the passenger seat.

"Dedrick. What's going on with you? Why are you acting clingy? It's like you're constantly wanting to see me. What's up with that?"

Clingy? Isn't that what boyfriends and girlfriends do?

"Forgive if I'm doing this relationship thing wrong, Brittany. But – "

"Relationship?" She laughed and shook her head. "That's

not what this is. I don't do relationships. No nigga has ever wanted one from me, so I don't expect them. Especially not someone like you. You and I are so...different."

"Different how? I don't care. I like you, Brittany." I looked her dead in her eyes, licking my lips as I admired her beauty. Even without the makeup and designer clothes, she was beautiful. I just wanted her to see herself through my eyes. "I want you to...to like me back. I know I'm not the cool kid on the block like all the other guys you know, but I'm...I'm a good person."

Confused, Brittany shook her head. "I like you, Dedrick. Just as a friend. I don't do anything past friendships."

So, why did we have sex?

"Brittany. I hope I'm not being too forward in saying this, but you're the girl I prayed for. Every night I would look at your picture and wonder if I'd ever get a chance to be with you." I left out the part about me masturbating to her picture, because I didn't want her to think I was weird. But, everything else I was saying was true. I wasn't the most religious person, but I used most of my conversations with God to ask him to bring her to me. Then, I proceeded to fulfilling my sexual desires. That had been my nightly ritual for about a year now, if not longer.

A small smile spread across Brittany's face, showing her dimples. "No man has ever said anything that sweet to me, Dedrick. To be honest, all guys ever see when they see me is a fat ass, and they just wanna hit. I've never had one want to take his time with me. I'm not sure how to even respond to that."

"Respond by saying yes. Let me court you." I grabbed her hand and put it up to my lips, to kiss. Her small hand smelt of Dove soap and tasted like a slice of Heaven. "Will you do me the honors of letting me date you? I want to show you what you've been deserving your entire life."

Without saying a word, Brittany leaned over in her seat, and unbuckled my pants, taking my meaty pole in her mouth. She didn't say the word "yes", but I sure hoped that this wasn't her way of saying no, either.

Chapter Fifteen

DOMINO BLACK

*A*fter moving all Bai's stuff back in the house, I ran her a nice bath in my Jacuzzi tub and let the soft sounds of old school R&B play on my stereo system. Learning about that shit that her ex did to her still had me fucked up, and although I wasn't the one who did it to her, I felt like I needed to make up for it. Yeah, I killed that nigga, but after talking to her, I realized she had some issues that we'd have to move past, thanks to that pussy nigga, and his death wasn't gon' make that shit just disappear. He fucked my girl up mentally, and I hated that, because I was supposed to make sure nothing or nobody brought her harm or stress. Only lame motherfuckers raped women, 'cuz they couldn't get pussy on their own. Swear, that man was lucky I couldn't bring his dead ass back to life, just to kill him again.

I was in my home study, finishing up some paperwork,

when an email from Tierra's stupid ass popped up. It was a picture of an ultrasound, but the bitch was on some other shit if she thought I believed it was hers for one minute. There was no name on the left-hand side – it was blurred out. I quickly deleted the email, and by the time I finished my work, Bailee was stepping out of the tub, coming toward me looking sexy as fuck. With nothing on, she was the baddest bitch in the world to me. And that's why I had no reason to fuck around on her; she gave a nigga everything I needed. These musty bitches couldn't compare to my baby, and although I never thought I'd say that shit about a female, I was proud to have her by my side. This being in love shit...it wasn't as bad as it seemed.

I licked my lips, admiring just how sick her body was. She had not one ounce of fat on her, and her skin was as smooth as chocolate.

"Come here." I summoned her to sit on my lap, as she wrapped herself in a towel. "You smell good as fuck, baby." Nibbling on her neck and ear made my dick brick up, and in no time, I had her doggy-style on the floor of my study, crying out my name, and making promises that I knew she'd keep, like having my baby and carrying my last name.

Bailee's pussy was drenching wet, so a nigga only lasted a few minutes before I shot my cum all inside of her. I was too fucking lazy to make it to the bed, so we laid on the floor and fell asleep, cradled in each other's arms. She had a nigga feeling soft as a motherfucker, but that was cool, because if I was gon' be soft for anybody, it was gon' be her. Bailee

Rodgers had changed me for the better, and from that moment, I vowed to myself to be the motherfucker she needed, because losing her just wasn't an option.

*T**he next day...*
Sitting across from Tatianna and James Montclair, I didn't know who the fuck to slap first. Probably Tatianna. She was the one who suggested a meeting with a "mogul who could make us lots of money", but she never dropped the name. I agreed to the meeting, only because I was about my check, but I should've known not to follow her ass up. Now that this old-ass, grease monkey, wanna-be King of Zamunda ass nigga was in my office again, I felt compelled to shoot him between the eyes for the way he disrespected me the first time I let him through these doors, and for having the audacity to come to my place of business again. The only thing stopping me from grabbing my pistol was Bailee. My baby wasn't here, but I knew if she was, she'd tell a nigga to relax. So that's what the fuck I was trying to do.

"Mr. Black, meet Mr. Montclair. He's the business mogul with a genius idea that I was telling you about. He's got a plan that will set The Black Palace apart from all other clubs." Tatianna beamed like the fucking sun when she spoke about this cat. He could fool her, but not me. His ass was two seconds away from getting the fuck out of my space. And if she wanted to go with him, she could get the boot as well. I was sick of her shit, too.

James reached out to shake my hand, but I smacked that shit. "Don't fucking violate my personal space, bruh. Fuck you doing here, again?"

"I've got an offer you can't refuse, Domino. May I sit down?"

"No. You fucking can't." I turned to Tatianna, who had made herself too goddamn comfortable in the chair across from me. "Fuck you bring this nigga in here for? He must not have told you he tried to get me before? The nigga is a snake, and I ain't working with him or his nasty ass liquor. Fuck him." I spoke just as if that motherfucker wasn't standing across from me, and I didn't give a fuck. "Escort your mother-fucking self out," I said to James, as I grabbed a stack of papers from the corner of my desk and began reviewing them. They weren't shit but bills, but looking at bills was more interesting to me than dealing with this damn shark.

When I saw that neither of them were moving, I took my pistol from out my drawer and pointed it right at that old nigga. "Get the fuck out of my office before my office is the last place yo' old pussy ass sees. Fucking whack ass nigga."

I took the safety off to show them I wasn't fucking around with either of them.

James must've finally gotten the hint because he grabbed that big ass briefcase of his and ran out the door like some-body who had heartburn, indigestion, upset stomach, and diarrhea.

"You. Bring your stupid ass over here." I barked at Tatianna, who was looking like she was on the verge of a nervous breakdown. "How the fuck you know that nigga, and why would you bring him here?"

"He's a smart businessman, Domino. He just wants to – "

"I don't give a fuck what he wants. That nigga shows up at my club one more time and he's going to meet his maker. You too."

"Fine." She rolled her eyes, like I was supposed to give a fuck that she had an attitude. She had me fucked up, though. "Is there anything you need from me, or can I leave? All that just gave me a headache."

"Yeah, you gave me a fucking headache too, with this bull-shit. Call Sunshine in here. Then go the fuck home."

When Sunshine or Camiyah, whichever the fuck you wanted to call her, walked her chubby ass in here, I immediately interrogated her ass. "You took that test yet?"

I told the hoe she had a couple of weeks to produce a paternity test for me proving that Davion was her child's father. I haven't gotten shit yet.

"Davion doesn't want a test, Domino."

Laughing, I shook my head. "That's a motherfucking lie, alright. Don't forget that we both made it out the same nutsack. I know my brother. And he ain't raising no baby that he didn't get tested. You hiding something?"

"Not at all." She shook her head and smiled, then took a seat in one of the chairs in my office.

"Stand the fuck up. I don't want yo' sweaty booty in my chairs."

Sucking her crooked ass teeth, she stood up. "Things are

good between Davion and me. I mean, I *am* the one taking care of him."

She was right, but that didn't mean she was being honest about who her baby belonged to. That just proved that she was willing to nurse a nigga back to health, in hopes of him taking care of her when he recovered. Camiyah couldn't fool me. I'd done all my research on her after the day she stepped to me about being Baby D's baby's mama.

She had no family. Her mom was a hoe, and her dad was one of those pitiful motherfuckers roaming the streets, begging niggas for a dollar so he could get a hit. She lived in the projects and had no way out except for my brother, so if she thought for one minute that she was gon' sit there and trap him, she had another thing coming. I was gon' dead that shit before it got any further.

"I love him, Domino. Davion is so misunderstood; the past couple of weeks since his injury have made us grow closer. Your brother is safe in my care."

"I didn't ask you about his safety. I asked you about that baby's paternity, and until you can produce it for me, you can consider yourself out of here."

A blank expression covered her face but I wasn't changing my mind. I didn't like manipulative people, and if I felt there was somebody in my camp on some bullshit, I'd get them out with a quickness. And she smelled as foul as a lump of shit.

Chapter Sixteen
BAILEE RODGERS

Today was the day we were starting to take clients at work, and I was excited as hell. My instructors had this little area for us set up like a real beauty parlor, which was dope. Each stylist – well, student – had our own chair, shampoo bowl, and shelf of products we could use on the clients' hair. None of us had no idea who our clients were, because they booked through the school, and none of us would make much money, since we only got to keep twenty percent of our earnings, but we were all excited to be one step closer to making our dreams come true.

As I waited for my two o'clock appointment, who was my first of the day, I decided to scroll through my Instagram news feed. Shivers went down my spine as I saw posts from Tyler's funeral, which was currently happening. I followed a few people who apparently knew him, and had gone to pay their respects.

What caught my eye the most was that in one of the funeral pictures, I saw not only Rhyan, but also the chick who he'd taken pictures with at whatever baby shower had gone down. She was photographed beside his mom, proving that he lied when he told me it was a friend of his and not his baby on the way. What pregnant friend would be sitting beside your mom at your funeral?

I saw a picture of Landon and Tas there, and I had to roll my eyes. Tas had bugged me about going to the funeral, but I told her I wouldn't feel comfortable. I never told her about what he did to me, and didn't plan on it either. Our relationship was so rocky that I wasn't sure if she'd believe me or not.

"I'm here for a two o'clock appointment with Bailee." A familiar voice said from behind me.

When I turned around, I was facing Sapphire, which was awkward as hell. I wanted to fight her for trying my man at the club that night, but I also wanted to thank her for doing him dirty, because had she not, I may not have ever gotten him.

"Wow, I didn't realize you were the Bailee my appointment was with."

Yeah fucking right. Sapphire was manipulative, so I was sure she'd scheduled an appointment with me on purpose, just to try to get in my head about Domino.

"You can have a seat." I ignored her dumb statement, and

put the black cape around her neck. "What is it that you want done, Sapphire?"

"I think I'll get a perm rod set. I always got compliments from my ex when I wore my hair that way. He always said it brought out my best features. Ouch!"

I burned that bitch with a flat iron on her neck, causing her to jump out my chair, because I knew she was referencing Domino, trying to be funny. "What did you do that for, Bailee? Oh my God!"

All the girls who were in my class laughed, because they knew just as much as Sapphire should've known, that I didn't play about my man. With everybody snickering at her and no one taking her side, she stormed out of the appointment just as quickly as she'd come in. I couldn't believe she tried me, but I planned to tell my sister to tell her little friend not to fuck with me anymore, or she'd get something worse next time. Bitch.

A few days later...

Janay, Celine, and I had decided to meet up for lunch, since we rarely got any girl time anymore. "I missed you guys," I whined, giving both my girls hugs as we got comfortable at Longhorn Steakhouse.

"Mamacita, you're glowing!" Celine winked at me, but I quickly shook my head. I was happy, but not glowing in the way she'd referenced. No babies over here.

"Don't jinx me with a baby, bitch! I'm just happy. What

y'all been up to? How are you guys doing? I feel like we never get to talk anymore."

"School, chica. And trying to keep my mind of Davion. I did kind of meet someone new, but I don't want to speak on it just yet." Celine looked away for a second, then refocused her attention back to us. I couldn't read her expression, so I didn't know if she was feeling down or not. Either way, I was glad she had at least met someone new; hopefully Davion's entitled, arrogant behind would be out of her system soon.

"And I've been chilling, just getting this money. I still can't believe you left me at Tony Marshall's house." Janay rolled her eyes and took a sip of her Sprite, then poked her lip out. "I got a lot of money that night, though. And my boo came through after that, so I was good. You ain't shit as a wingman, though."

"Yeah, well, that's because my man came through and shut shit down." I chuckled, thinking about how Domino interrupted that listening party just to find me. Crazy ass.

"I don't see how you deal with a nigga as crazy as Domino," Janay laughed, shaking her head. "Y'all were made for each other, 'cuz your ass is missing some screws too. I'm surprised y'all don't beat each other's asses every day."

"Who's to say we don't?" I teased, making my girls laugh.

It was good to spend time with Celine and Janay. Especially Janay. Out of our trio, she was the one who barely had any time for partying or hanging out. Then, when she did have time, she was often low on funds, so she'd bow out. I was happy that wasn't the case today. I didn't even have anything bad to say about her attire today. Sometimes, she would have on really worn clothing and shoes, so we'd always fix her up. But today she looked super cute, wearing a black halter romper with pink flowers all over it. Celine had complimented me on my glow, but she needed to be sending that compliment to Janay.

Maybe it was because she finally had a man that she was looking and dressing better. She'd been hanging with Weezy lately, and although I didn't know many details, I thought they were a perfect match. Well, other than the fact that his ass was a married man. "You might wanna be careful with Weezy, Janay. I don't think his divorce is final yet."

I didn't think he'd filed at all, but I wanted to give my girl some hope.

"He's working on that."

Cool. I left it at that, because she seemed a little defensive when she replied. I understood, though, because I hated when people gave me warnings about Domino, as if I didn't know my man was crazy as hell.

The rest of our lunch went pretty smoothly, because we left men off our menu. There was certainly enough to catch up on between the three of us, but I couldn't lie, I was ready to get home to my man.

A few days later... Domino and I had just landed in Miami, and I was excited to unwind for a couple of days and lay up on the beach with my favorite guy. Of course, he had to handle business while we were here, but I planned to take full advantage of the last few days of summer this weekend with my boo.

Sometimes, when I stared at him, it was hard for me to believe he was all mine. I was currently having one of those "pinch me is this real" moments as I watched him change into his swim trunks, so we could go play on the beach for a few hours. His muscles looked even more ripped than they were when I first met him, and now that he had a tattoo of my name across his back, he looked even more delectable without a shirt on.

"Damn, baby. You look good as fuck in that lil' bikini shit. Got me wanting to keep you in the room and do some things to you." He licked his lips sexily, admiring how I looked in my new all white two-piece.

I had to admit, I did look damn good, especially for someone who didn't work out often. I did yoga in my spare time, just to keep busy, but it wasn't something I did on the regular. I guess I was just blessed.

Gripping my ass, Domino pulled me closer to him, bringing me in for a kiss that was so arousing I almost got pregnant. His tongue felt so good going down my throat that when our lips finally unlocked, I could still feel him on me.

When we got to the beach, all eyes were on us as we picked our spot to lay out on. I knew I'd cause attention since my bikini was a thong one, showing all my assets. But the bitches were staring hard at Domino, making me almost catch a case. I had a rude nigga, though. And I loved that shit.

"You need something?" He asked one bitch who was damn near salivating on herself as we walked past.

She shook her head like she was embarrassed. "No."

"Then give me my motherfucking face back, bitch. Looking like E.T.'s cousin."

The dumb girl didn't even seem fazed by the fact that Dom had insulted her. She was still grinning in his face, just happy he'd spoken to her, I guess. Thirty ass.

"You ever thought about getting married?" Domino asked me out the blue, once we were comfortable in our beach chairs, letting the water cover our feet.

"Of course. Every girl wants to get married. Do you ever think about marriage?"

"Sometimes. I mean, it ain't no dream for a man like it is for y'all. Y'all motherfuckers pop out the pussy dreaming about your wedding day. The only time I've ever thought about marriage was with you."

I didn't know what to say. "You think about marrying me?"

"You hard of hearing or something? 'Cuz I swear that's just what the fuck I said."

I splashed him with some of the water. "Shut up, nigga! All this bullshit you've taken me through, you better marry me. And give me some really pretty, chocolate babies."

"I hope they look like me and not your family. You cute as fuck, but I don't know what happened with the genes in your family 'cuz your sister ain't hitting on shit."

Rude.

Just knowing that he was even thinking long-term with me

was making me feel all giddy inside. "I think it's finally time for you to meet my parents." I'd been putting it off long enough. The one time I'd set it up, it didn't happen because I got in an argument with him in the car. My parents knew I was living with him, but hadn't come to our house to meet him or anything. I didn't expect my mom to, but I did want to introduce him to my dad at least.

"I can do that, baby." Domino leaned over and gave me another kiss, and had there not been kids on this beach with us, I would've probably sat right on his dick and rode him all night long.

*T*he next day...
"I love this building, baby! I'm so excited." It was my first time seeing the building, because when I came with him to Miami the last time, I was in the hotel while he met with the realtor.

Now that the spot was officially his, the work had begun on both the outside and inside to make it to his liking. The outside of the building read "The Black Palace Miami" in gold letters, and so far, the inside was coming along nicely.

Just like in the Columbia location, there was a huge bar area, and poles all over the dance floor. There were also cages in this location, too.

"The girls can climb out of the cages and land right on the pole, then slide down," Daria, the realtor, explained.

That was pretty dope.

"Everything looks good, Daria. How soon you think every-thing will be ready?" Domino asked, while his eyes continued to scan the place.

"Well, Mr. Black, after you hold your interviews today, half the work will be done. We can probably have a grand opening by October 5th."

That was only a few weeks away. Excitement filled my man's face, and I was so proud of him for manifesting his dream. I was proud to be the woman who stood beside him while he expanded his brand.

After walking around the club a little more, we had a quick lunch at a nearby restaurant, and then headed back to the club to get the tryouts started. Domino had posted on his social media accounts about the auditions for dancers, and since he was pretty well known, word spread like wildfire. There were hundreds of girls lined up when we got back to the club, some I knew would make the cut simply based on their appearances, while there were others who I knew wouldn't. Domino was a man who was big on looks and hygiene, and some of these girls smelled and looked straight out of a zoo.

"Go home." Domino said to one chick as we skimmed the line before opening the doors. "I'm not hiring you. Don't waste your time."

My mouth fell as the girl's smile faded upon him telling her to go home. "Fuck you too!"

"Looks like your mama fucked a monkey, and that's how she got you. Take your ugly ass on!"

"Baby, stop! Be nice." I laughed, because his brashness was funny, but he didn't have to be so rude.

Domino stopped at the next female in line, and I already knew he was going to say some harsh shit. "You. You deliver toys at Christmas?"

The girl looked confused and embarrassed. "No, sir."

"Then why the fuck you look like Santa Claus? You can go. I don't need your ass breaking my poles. And you." He turned to another girl and pointed at her. "What's your favorite fish?"

"Umm, sushi?"

"I can tell. You smell like it. Get the fuck out of here."

A few girls in the line snickered, but they tried to keep it on the low so he didn't come for them, too. He dismissed a few more of the girls before giving them a chance, and the rest, he let in. We watched them dance in groups of three on the stage, and we rated them from zero to ten, with ten being the highest, based on looks, performance, and overall personality. Domino wanted to hire only the baddest in Miami, and after watching all the girls dance and making our decisions, I knew we'd picked the top candidates.

"Thanks for letting me have a hand in your business, baby." I kissed him passionately, when we got back to our hotel room.

"Don't do that, Bai."

"Do what?" I was so confused...

"Get me all horny and shit, knowing we gotta catch that flight in the morning."

I laughed and gave my man another kiss, this time sucking

his juicy bottom lip a little longer than normal. As badly as I wanted to give him some tonight, he was right. Our flight was leaving in less than five hours, and we hadn't packed up much of anything in the room.

The next day...

When we made it back to Columbia, all I wanted to do was rest. This weekend had tired me out because in Miami, we were on the go nonstop. I had class in the morning, then had booked a girl's appointment for five o'clock tomorrow afternoon, so tomorrow was going to be busy as well.

Domino left me to go hang with his boys, Terrell and Roman, which was cool because I kind of wanted to be alone anyway. Nothing against him, but I needed the me-time. Plus, I wanted a chance to take this pregnancy test I'd purchased in peace. I couldn't hide shit from Dom, because he was so in tune with my body, my needs, and my actions, so I was surprised I'd been able to hide this from him for so long.

I had never taken a pregnancy test before, but I read that it was more accurate if I used fresh pee, so I hadn't eaten or drank anything since breakfast, which was hours ago. My heart raced as I ripped the test from the packet, and read the instructions. They were pretty simple, but I didn't want to risk messing anything up.

Once I let my urine hit the stick, I was careful not to tilt it so I didn't alter the results. I wiped myself and sat it down on the bathroom counter as I washed my hands and prayed. I prayed that it was negative, only because I wasn't ready to be someone's mother. I wanted to embark on this journey when I had a shop up and running, and established clientele, not when I was in school to obtain a cosmetology degree. A baby would push things so much further behind. Not only was I not ready for a baby, but depending on when I got pregnant, it could've been Tyler's baby. I would hate to have to bring a baby into this world who was a result of a rape with my ex-boyfriend. That seemed like the hardest thing in the world to do, and although I prayed that wasn't the case for me, it was a possibility.

After waiting about two more minutes, I decided to peek at the test, and the blue plus sign showed me all that I was hoping not to see. I sat on the toilet and bawled, because for once, God did not answer my prayers.

Chapter Seventeen

WEEZY

on't laugh when I say this, alright? But, a nigga's been going to therapy, and it's been helping me out. A lot. I kind of felt like a bitch for saying that shit, but it was the truth. I had some deep rooted issues that stemmed from my upbringing, and besides Janay, I had no one else but the therapist to talk to about it. Shit was refreshing.

I can't say I wouldn't done this on my own, though. This was all shorty's doing. Janay and I have been kicking it real tough lately, and after I opened up to her about everything, and she suggested I seek therapy. Normally, a nigga would laugh and say that therapy was some white people shit, but the person she referred me to was actually down to earth and made me feel comfortable. I still haven't told my homeboys I'd been going, but at least I was learning to feel better about myself.

Lena had my self-esteem all fucked up. My therapist, Dr. Taylor, explained to me that Lena was using reverse psychology on me in order to lower my self-esteem. Basically, since I cheated on her first, she was using that incident from years ago to manipulate me into accepting everything she was doing to me. The physical abuse she always uses on me is because she feels like she needs something to control, and she wanted it to be me. But, Dr. Taylor wanted me to find my fucking voice, so that she couldn't do that shit anymore.

That's the part I was working on. I needed to stand up to her, but it always seemed easier just to try to numb the pain with my weed and molly than to face what was going on. I know it ain't right, but drugs were my coping mechanism; now that I had Janay on my team, she was able to fill in some of that void, so I didn't feel like I needed my smokes as much.

I was staring at her cute ass sleep right now, and I'd come to the conclusion that she was the baddest female a nigga had ever laid eyes on. With smooth caramel skin and thick, black hair to compliment her pretty, almond shaped eyes, Janay was damn sure one of God's best creations. I hated that life was so hard for her; I swear I wanted to just take all her money problems away. I didn't know what it was like for a family to depend on me for financial support, but I did know what it was like being down on my luck and desperate, and that's why I told myself I was gon' do whatever I had to do so my girl didn't have to work a full time job and a half time hoe job while going to school.

"Good morning, beautiful." I smiled at Janay as she opened her eyes and yawned.

We were at a thirty-dollar motel, since that was all I could afford at the moment. I was out of a job, so money was mad tight for me, and I didn't want her spending any of her coins on a room for us.

"Good morning," she replied back. "I forgot where I was for a second."

"Yeah, I know it's not the nicest spot, but – "

Janay put her fingers up to my lips to close them. "Hush, Weezy. It's fine. As long as I'm with you, it's fine."

See, that was the type of shit I liked about her. She was appreciative of my efforts. Most bitches didn't give a fuck about the fact that I was broke – they still wanted it all and would rather knock a nigga down who was trying, than to help build him up. Shit, Lena was the reason I got fired from my last job, yet she didn't want to help build me up as I looked for a new one. Instead, she told me I was fucking worthless and a waste of space. In the same breath, she'd threaten to kill me if I ever tried to leave her. So, I never knew whether her ass wanted me or not. But now, I was at the point where I no longer had a fuck to give. If she wanted me, that was her problem, because I been off that.

Knock! Knock!

"I didn't realize room cleaning came this early." Janay commented, sitting up in the small twin bed.

"Me neither." I walked over to the door and when I opened it, I instantly regretted it. I tried to close the door, but because Lena was almost triple my size, she was able to break the damn hinges off the door.

I didn't even have to ask how she'd found me, because it was obvious she'd either followed me or checked the bank statement. "Lena. I can explain."

"Explain it to my taser!" She whipped out her taser and before I could move out of her way, I felt myself fall to the ground, convulsing, due to the electric shock sent through my body with her taser.

She got Janay next, which made me feel bad as fuck because I was supposed to protect her at all times.

The next day...
After the shit that went down yesterday at the motel with Lena, I decided I was gon' have to get the fuck away from her, and going down the street to a motel wasn't good enough for my escape. She was fucking mental, and putting Janay in danger wasn't something I wanted to do, 'cuz shorty was cool as fuck. Janay suggested that I ask Dom if I could move in with him for a while, just 'til I got on my feet. She was supposed to put a bug in Bailee's ear about asking him, and hopefully she did, because this was already some tough shit I was gon' have to ask my nigga, but I was ready to do it. Hell, the worst he could say was no.

When Lena and the twins left the house, I decided to make my escape. She took the keys to my car after finding me with Janay a second time last night, so I had to call an Uber.

Once I got to Dom's crib, I rang his doorbell, with all my belongings in gray, plastic Dollar Tree bags, hoping those motherfuckers didn't tear. Not that there were many things I had in there, anyway. Lately, anytime I went shopping, Lena would take my new shit and sell it on the Facebook market, because she didn't think I deserved to have new clothes since I barely contributed to the household. Don't get a nigga wrong – I had money coming in. Unemployment checks. But, it wasn't much, compared to hers, since she was working every day. She worked in healthcare, working from home three out of the five days a week, just so she could keep even more tabs on my ass.

I missed working, because at least when I was working, Lena treated me like a man, except when I was out there doing dirt. She respected me more when I was bringing home more money than she was, but if she really cared about me making money, why the fuck did she go out of her way to get me fired? I could barely look for a new job, 'cuz the bitch changed the Wi-Fi password and refused to give it to me. So I couldn't even look for one online, when I was home.

Since my boy was taking a while to get to the door, I rang the doorbell again.

"Who the fuck is it?" Dom roared through the door.

"Me, man. Weezy!"

Seconds later, the door opened, and I could tell from his surprised expression that Janay hadn't given Bailee the head's up, or maybe Bailee didn't get to ask Dom if it was okay. Either way, my nigga wasn't expecting me.

"Fuck you doing here with all them plastic bags, bruh? You went grocery shopping or some shit? And don't ever rush me to come to the door. You see my cars, you know I'm home. Acting like you the feds or some shit."

Laughing, I shook my head and ignored his last statement. "This is all my shit from Lena's house, bruh. I was wondering if I could chill with you here for a bit, just 'til I got my shit together."

"Here?" Domino scowled, as I nodded my head.

I didn't show up at his parents' house, the one where Baby D and Dedrick still lived. Instead, I was at his house, which was the place he even hated telling people about, because he didn't like to be bothered with certain shit.

I nodded my head to answer Domino's question and he immediately shook his head. "Nah, motherfucker. Not *this* crib. My bitch lives with me, bruh, and she be walking around here in those smedium shorts and shit. I don't wanna catch you looking and have to rip your eyeballs out."

"Swear to God, I won't look at your girl, man. I'm not interested."

"You saying my bitch ugly?"

Laughing, I shook my head. "Nah, bruh. Bailee's beautiful. I got something else on my radar, though. I would never disrespect you like that. I ain't trying to fuck your girl, Dom."

"We can work something out at my parents' crib. Maybe you can use my old room for a bit. I'll make sure Dedrick's nerdy ass cleans up all that – "

Interrupting my boy, I shook my head. "Lena knows where

that house is, player. She doesn't know where this one is. She don't know shit about this spot. Please, homie. I'm desperate." I was trying not to sound like a bitch and cry, but I was almost at that point. I couldn't take Lena popping up on me and beating my ass anywhere else. Shit was embarrassing.

"Bring yo' ass in, man. And if Lena followed you and is about to start some shit, I'm taking her big ass out with my AK." Domino shut the door behind me, and pointed to the AK that stayed in his foyer. I knew he was serious, so I hoped Lena didn't follow me. She wasn't a good wife, but I damn sure didn't want her dead, because then I'd be responsible for those fucking kids that I just knew weren't mine.

Dom lit a blunt and handed it to me, then grabbed a cigar for himself. "Talk to me, motherfucker. What's going on?"

Similar to how I'd done in therapy with Dr. Taylor, I started from the top, explaining how Lena had been on my ass for years, even after she cheated back. Then I told him about the abuse. Just as I expected him to, he laughed at first, not realizing I was serious 'til I showed him some scars and shit. Then, he offered me one of his guest bedrooms and a temporary position at The Black Palace, which I happily accepted.

"Under two conditions. First, close yo' fucking eyes whenever Bailee is in the room."

I would've laughed had I thought he was playing, but I knew my boy well enough to know he was dead ass serious. He really didn't want anybody looking Bailee's direction, but he had nothing to worry about with me.

"Second condition." Domino cleared his throat and looked

me in the eyes sternly. "Put the fucking drugs down. Pipes, rocks, powder...all that shit, man. I got enough shit the police could be on my ass about, and I'll be damned if I add you to my list. Don't make me kick your ass, Renard. You thought Lena gave you a black eye, I'll make that shit purple."

Ignoring his threats, I dapped my boy up. "Thanks, man." I went upstairs to one of his guest bedrooms so I could get comfortable, and all I could do was hope everything worked out like it was supposed to for me in the end. I was tired of living my life as Lena's slave. And quite honestly, I was tired of leaning on drugs and lean to numb my pain. I wanted to feel fucking regular, so I had no problem with my nigga's house rules. I just hoped Lena's ass wouldn't find out where I was, 'cuz I already knew Dom would kill her ass on sight. I wished she'd just let me be.

Chapter Eighteen

DAVION "BABY D" BLACK

*E*ver since my injury on the field, Camiyah had been sticking by her word and taking care of a nigga. Her and that loud ass, always crying ass baby weren't supposed to be in my dorm, but since when did I give a fuck about rules? They spent the night with me some nights at my dorm, and other nights, we'd spent at my parents' house.

I know when I agreed to her lil' comment about us being family, I was just doing it to fuck Celine up, but if anybody was treating me like family at the time when I was at my lowest, it was her. Domino looked out, because although he fired Camiyah, he still laced my bank account every week, but Camiyah was the one taking me back and forth to doctor's appointments and shit. The only thing she didn't do for me is let me get high, and I was on edge, wanting a hit.

"Is there anything I can do for you, daddy?" Camiyah

asked, walking into the bedroom with Camia in her arms. We were at my crib, and she'd just finished cooking us some lunch. She surprised the fuck out of me, because when she asked if I wanted spaghetti, I was sure she was gon' be heating up some fucking Spaghetti-O's or some shit. But nah, Camiyah was a really good cook. I guess since she damn near raised herself, she had to learn all that domestic shit early.

I was really surprised that she was a good mom. This whole time I'd been fucking with her, I thought since she was a stripper, she was one of those dirty hoes who wouldn't be able to do shit but shake her ass. I'm man enough to admit that I was wrong.

Camiyah told me her motivation for being a good mom to Camia came from the horrible excuse of a mother she had, and I could respect that. Shorty kept her daughter clean, fed, and laughing, and she also made time to do that lil' mommy shit with her, like reading stories and singing nursery rhymes.

"Nah. I'm good. Come sit with me."

Camiyah sat on the bed, wearing one of my old high school t-shirts and a pair of mismatched socks. I surprised her and took the baby out of her arms, just to give her a quick break. I honestly don't know what's come over me, but being nice to Camiyah had been on my to-do list lately. Other shit on my to-do list was to get this damn paternity test. I hoped she didn't think I'd forgotten.

"When do you wanna get this test done, Camiyah? Didn't you say if the test came back positive, Domino would give you your job back?"

She nodded her head slowly. "I don't have the money for a test right now, Davion. I just don't."

"I got it." I didn't plan on telling her how much money was in my account, because I didn't want her to make a habit of asking me for shit, since technically, she wasn't my woman. But the test, I'd pay for, because the anticipation was killing me. Secretly, I could feel myself falling in love with lil' Camia, and I didn't want a Weezy situation headed my way; basically, I didn't want to find out later on that the baby wasn't mine. Didn't want to be tricked into doing all this shit for a kid just to find out years later that it had a real daddy somewhere else. Shit like that would send a nigga straight to jail for life, 'cuz I'd be on Camiyah's ass with a sledgehammer.

"Ok. We can take it, Davion. I'll call and set up the appointment."

The fact that she was so cool with doing it made me feel like she was pretty positive Camia was mine. For her sake, she'd better hope that was the case. Not saying I was feeling her or anything, because at the end of the day, she was a hoe, whether she liked it or not, but if the baby was mine I'd take care of her.

Speaking of babies, I heard from that dumb bitch, Shanay again. I blocked her number the first time she hit me, and today, she'd texted me from another number. That dumb ass little girl had sent a picture of her fucking belly, as if I wouldn't kick that shit in if I had known her location.

I was saving all that shit for my lawyer, though. Denise told me I needed to prove that nobody was forcing the lil' bitch to fuck with me, and to see if I could prove that she had lied about her age. She wasn't sure if that would get this lil' charge off completely, but it would help lessen the blow. So, I spent the next couple of minutes going through my phone, screen shotting conversations I had with the hoe and sending them to Denise. I'll be damned if I let a lil' freshman bitch get me caught up and ruin my fucking life.

A few days later... I'd decided to spend tonight without Camiyah and Camia so I could catch up on my school work and shit. They'd been taking up a lot of my time, and now it was time to get back on the grind so I could focus on the important shit – football. My ankle was slowly healing, and I predicted I'd be able to play again within the next few weeks. It was a rule at USC that our GPA had to be at a 2.75 or higher the week of each game we played in, and since I'd been slacking off a bit, with everything else going on, I knew I needed to spend some time in the books today.

When I walked into the Thomas Cooper library, I felt a pair of eyes on me. Wondering who the fuck was staring me down so hard, I turned around to see Celine, and I swear she looked like she was leaking through her panties, yet at the same time, nervous as fuck.

So, of course I had to fuck with her. Wanted to see what was on her mind. "What's up? Long time no see." I walked toward where she was sitting, buried in a psychology text-book. "How you been?"

"Good. Busy. Now, adios." She slammed her book shut and tried to get up, but I grabbed her arm to stop her. "Get off me, Davion! You made it clear you didn't want me, papi! So don't try to talk to me now. El Cabron!"

"Look, I don't know who the fuck Cabron is but you better listen to me, bitch! You ain't done with me until I say so! Fuck you think this is, Celine?" I had a steady grip on her arm, and although I saw tears in the corners of her eyes, I didn't give a shit. She had me fucked up, wanting to show out in the library and shit. I wasn't even gon' say shit to her, but since she wanted to act up, I was gon' give her ass what she wanted.

I knew just the thing to tame her – my long john. With a tight grip still on her arm, I walked her to the elevator and we rode down to the first floor.

"Why are we going down here, papi? What's gotten into you?" She reached for the emergency button, but I hit her hand.

"Nothing yet. And stop acting like you don't want me, girl." I laughed. "I'm about to be in you in a minute. You obviously forgot how good I made you feel, so you must need a reminder so you can stop tripping on me like you're fucking crazy."

We got off the elevator, and I pushed her in the bathroom, then locked the door behind us. Just as I knew she would, she was trying to cover herself as if I'd never seen her body before. I moved her hands, bringing her closer to me, until she finally caved in.

Grabbing her by her chin, I squeezed it and whispered in her ear as the other hand slid down to get her pussy right. That shit wasn't as wet as I wanted it, so I stirred the pot a lil' bit, 'til my fingers became soaked. "The next time you want some fucking dick, just ask, alright?"

She was shaking her head, but none of that shit mattered to me, 'cuz she wasn't moving my hand. Celine knew she liked it. After moaning for several seconds, she finally spoke. "But, papi, you have a...a...familia."

Jamming my fingers in her box more roughly, her breathing quickened and her moans became louder.

"None of that shit matters, alright? If you want some of this dick, I don't give a fuck who's around, you come get it." I pressed my body closer onto hers, so she could feel just how much she was making me brick up, with her sexy ass. "Do you want it? Yes or yes?"

"I...just...need...some...time."

"How much fucking time you need, bitch?" I was starting to get fed up with his hoe, man. I needed all the drugs in the world to deal with this stupid bitch. I was trying to throw her some dick, yet she wasn't taking it. She knew good and fucking well she had gold between her thighs, and a nigga just wanted to dig.

Catching me off guard, she laughed and pushed me away from her. "You haven't changed at all, Davion! Get away from me! Forever, por favor!"

The only reason I didn't box the bitch in the mouth is because she seemed like the type to call the pigs on a nigga eventually, and I didn't have no time for their asses at the moment. But Celine Gomez better watch her back, 'cuz no bitch on this earth was gon' get away with disrespecting me.

E ver since I've found that I was with child, all these pregnancy symptoms have been hitting me. *Hard.* Nausea. Drowsiness. Nothing about pregnancy was beautiful.

I never thought I'd say this, but I was extremely happy Domino was in Miami today without me, because I could take some time and process this pregnancy in peace. He and Weezy had gone for the two days to finish some things with the new location, and I was glad that he wasn't here to witness everything I was feeling. Before he left, I'd been hiding my morning sickness and tiredness, just so he wouldn't ask any questions or get suspicious. I knew if he found out I was carrying a child, he wouldn't let me do what I was about to do.

I pulled up to the abortion clinic, and the protestors damn near bum-rushed my car. They surrounded my vehicle with signs of Jesus, pictures of babies, and signs that read "Murderer".

"You're none of those things, Bailee. You're doing the right thing." My sister assured me, rubbing my back as I silently prayed for God to drop me one more sign that I was doing the right thing.

When one of the protestors jumped on the hood of my car, I thought that was it.

"Okay Tas. I'm ready."

I know it seems odd that my sister was joining me on this little event, but I didn't want to be here alone. Nor did I want to bring someone who would try to talk me out of it. My sister was one of the most anti-Domino women around, so I knew she wouldn't try to talk me out of aborting his baby.

"I still can't believe you're having an abortion done, Bailee."

"And I still can't believe you knew about Tyler's baby on the way and didn't tell me." I spat, hoping that would make her shut the hell up about what was going on in my uterus.

On the way here, she'd pestered me about why I missed Tyler's home going service, and I just went ahead and told her everything. Well, not everything, but about how he raped me and how I found out he had a child on the way. She claimed she'd just found out the day of the funeral, but I knew my sister had to have been lying. I didn't press the issue, though, because I truly no longer cared. Tyler was dead to me...literally.

"Bailee Rodgers. Here for a twelve o'clock appointment."

I signed in with the receptionist, while my sister took a seat in the lobby.

I joined Tasmine in the waiting area after completing all types of paperwork. She placed her hand over my knee, and told me to calm down.

Calm down? Bitch, I was about to murder my baby. You can't calm down from that. I had a million thoughts rushing through my mind, and none of them were good. I was fearful. I was regretful. And most of all, I was nervous about what Domino would do if he were to ever find out.

O *ne hour later...*
              After forcing me to listen to my baby's heart-beat, I was told to wait in the cold room for the doctor to come in and explain my options. *Options.* As if I had any. All I wanted to do was get rid of this child that could possibly be Tyler's, and move on with my life, without ever telling Domino or anyone besides my sister about this.

"So, Ms. Rodgers. Do you want the pill or the surgery?" The doctor walked in with a manilla folder, and sat down beside me. "You're not too far along; only seven weeks and four days, so if you wanted the series of pills, you could take them and do this in the comfort of your own home."

That sounded better than going through a surgical abortion, so I decided to go with that option. After saying a quick prayer, asking God and my unborn child to forgive me, I took the small white pill from the doctor and swallowed it. He sent me home with the other pill, and told me to take it tomorrow to finish the process. According to him, the pill I'd just started was breaking down the baby's limbs, and tomorrow's pill would completely terminate the pregnancy.

I didn't know how to feel once I left the abortion clinic. Prior to doing this, I knew I wasn't ready to be a mom. As I drove back to my parents' house to rest, I started wondering "what if". It was too late for that, though. Hopefully God would give me another chance, once I was completely ready and knew for sure that Domino was my child's father. I kept trying to convince myself that I'd done what was best, but the hole I felt in my heart didn't seem like it'd ever go away.

wo days later...
Domino was now back in town, so I had to act like everything was copacetic. Deep down, I was dying. I missed my baby so much. Just the thought of having a child that could have been half of me and half of the man I loved brought me to tears, because I'd diminished those chances, for now at least.

I was still bleeding and cramping like crazy from the two pills I'd taken, so Dom was catering to me the best way he could. He thought I was just having a heavy cycle this month.

"I'll be back, baby. Me and Weezy gotta go make some moves for the club. But when I come back, I'm gonna run you a bath and then let you suck my dick."

"*Let* me suck your dick?" I laughed, playfully hitting him on the arm as he placed a kiss on my forehead.

"Yep. Since a nigga can't get no pussy 'cuz you wanna be Bloody Mary and shit, I need to get my dick wet somehow. Shit, unless..."

"Unless what, nigga? I dare you to say it. I'll cut you." I grabbed a pair of scissors off the dresser beside me and held them to his dick.

"Bail, I swear to fucking God if you don't move those scissors from by my dick, I'm gonna – "

"You're gonna what?" I snipped the scissors and accidentally cut a piece of his pants off.

Laughing, he tackled me, laying me back on the bed and showering me with soft kisses all over my face. After letting me up for air, he changed his pants and left with Weezy, and I drifted off into a deep sleep. I just wanted this physical and emotional pain to be over, so I could get back to feeling like myself again, but that didn't look like it'd be happening anytime soon.

A few days later...
All the bleeding and cramping had finally stopped, and I'd been able to get back to school and also helping Domino plan the opening night for The Black Palace Miami. All the girls he'd offered jobs to accepted, and now the last thing he needed to do was hire bartenders and security guards. My baby had been working his ass off to make sure

that everything with his second location was perfect, so tonight, I just wanted us to have some fun. And there was no better place to have fun in Columbia than The Black Palace, because each week, the crowd got thicker, thanks to word of mouth and all the social media promotion him and his team put together.

Rocking my hips to the beat of YFN Lucci's hit, *In a Minute,* I danced alongside Janay as our men took shots of patron watching us. Janay seemed happier than she'd been in a while, and I guess Weezy was the reason behind that. I didn't get too much into their personal business, because Domino told me not to worry about nobody's relationship but mine, but from what I could see, they were good for each other.

"You know you the finest bitch in this club. Wanna come home with me?" A sexy voice whispered in my ear as I grinded my hips to the song.

"I can't. I have a boyfriend. And he's crazy as fuck, too. You might wanna walk away before he sees you talking to me." I laughed, and kissed Domino.

Simple shit like that made me smile. He never stopped flirting with me. He never stopped telling me how beautiful I was. The same way Domino got me back in July was how he was still working to keep me in September, and although we haven't been together long at all, our connection was so strong that I knew he was the one for me.

Just as we sat down to pop open the bottle of Ace of Spades that was waiting for us, Domino said he had to go check out something in the back, so he gave me a passionate kiss, leaving me with Janay and Weezy.

"Hurry back, sexy."

"I will," he promised, then he disappeared in the dark club.

Chapter Twenty

DAVION "BABY D" BLACK

"What the fuck are you doing back here, nigga? Coming to try to take some more cash?"

I didn't realize my brother saw me slide in the club and go in his office, but oh well, fuck it. I needed another hit and although he put some money in my account a few days ago, I needed more. I'd just found out that Camiyah's baby was mine, and I didn't know to cope with that shit. One minute I was cool with it; the next, I was mad as fuck and wanted to ring her neck for trapping me.

"I asked you a motherfucking question, Davion!" Domino got in my face like he was my fucking pops and pushed me hard, making me fall onto the couch in his office.

"Who the fuck you pushing, motherfucker? I came to get some money! And what?" I got back in his face, letting him know not to fuck with me. "You wanna sit here and pay Weezy, nigga! What about me? I'm your fucking blood!"

"Weezy works for me, nigga! You don't do shit."

I don't know if it was the anger, jealousy, or adrenaline pumping, but I knocked all that nigga's shit off his desk and flipped it over.

I instantly regretted it, though, because Dom came straight for my head, punching the fuck out of me. Here I was, with a sprained fucking ankle, getting my ass beat by my older brother. When he finally gave me some mercy and stopped throwing blows at me, he went into his safe and handed me a stack of hundreds.

"This what you want, nigga? You doing all this for some money for what? So you can get high? Answer me, motherfucker!"

"I just need it...to numb my pain, bruh." My lip was busted and bleeding, so it hurt to talk. "Please. After today, I won't use it anymore."

"After today, I don't give a fuck what you do." He threw the money at me, and I dashed to the floor like the true fiend I was to grab all the bills. "Get the fuck out of my office, Davion. And get the fuck out of mom and pop's crib. I better not catch you there, here, or any fucking where. You're dead to me."

His words hurt, but the money I'd just gotten was making everything better. I knew he didn't mean what he said. He never did. Domino was the typical oldest brother; he looked out for us, even when he didn't want to. So, although I was taking this money and doing what the fuck I wanted with it, I knew he wasn't going to turn his back on me. He was just mad at the moment.

*O*ne *hour later...*
          Snorting this white shit was the best feeling ever. All the anger I had for my brother, these bitches, and even this dumb ass baby laying beside me, went away when I did some lines.

Since Dom told me to get out of my parents' house, I decided to spend the night at Camiyah's run down house, only because I knew if I came over here, there would be somebody I could get some powder from. Camiyah lived in the hood, and not only was this shit quality, but I got it for the low low too.

"Davion! Davion, get up! The baby could've put this shit in her mouth!"

I felt Camiyah touching me, but my body was stuck; I couldn't move. That's how it felt every time I did a hit, and I loved that shit.

"Davion, you've gotta go. You can't stay here and do this. I can't allow it." Camiyah sat beside me as I was slowly coming down from my euphoria. She definitely knew how to blow a nigga's high with all that talking and shit. That's why I liked to be alone when I did my shit, so I could enjoy it without being interrupted by an annoying ass bitch.

"I ain't going no fucking where. You and that fucking baby can leave."

Wham!

Camiyah smacked me upside the head, but I didn't even have the energy to hit her back. I just laughed. Her lil' hit didn't hurt. I was a football player, had she forgotten? I took hits from motherfuckers my size and bigger, so a smack from a bitch didn't mean shit to me.

"Now, if I hit you back, I'd be wrong, right? Leave me the fuck alone, Camiyah." I wiped the residue from my nose and sealed the rest of my coke up for another day. Shit, who was I kidding? I'd be back in my stash by the end of the night.

Camiyah grabbed the bag from me and ran into her dirty ass kitchen to pour it down the drain. I didn't even stop her. I had more where that came from. And I money to buy more when I ran out of *that* stash.

"Either come suck my dick or leave me the fuck alone."

"Davion, we need to talk. You gotta stop doing this, baby. It's not healthy. What would your mom and – "

Wham!

"What my mom and dad think doesn't fucking matter, alright? They're dead! They fucking left me here, so fuck them! Fuck you and fuck that baby, too! I'm out!"

I got in my car and drove off, mad as fuck. Nobody understood me, and nobody would just let a nigga be! Everybody wanted to fuck with me, and at this point, I wanted to fuck everybody up!

. . .

he next day...
I went back to the roach motel I fucked that hoe that robbed me at, and she was right back there, on her knees in the parking lot, sucking some shrimp dick nigga off. I scooped her from off the ground and carried her to the room I'd gotten. I made her suck me and fuck me, then I kicked her Flava Flav looking ass out. I just wanted to be paid back, and since I knew she didn't have the bands she stole from me anymore, I got some free head and pussy out of her.

Right as I was about to be leaving, that nasty roach motel, Denise's number popped up on my screen.

"What's up?"

"Davion! I've got great news! Mr. Starkes and his family retracted all statements – she admitted she lied. You're clear!"

Word. I could hardly believe that shit, but a nigga was happy as fuck. I guess this is what feeling blessed felt like, 'cuz I couldn't handle anymore fucking drama or retarded shit headed my way. I hung up with Denise and decided to go stock up on my shit. Another week or so 'til I was back on that football field, *and* I was cleared from all this pedophile shit? Oh, a nigga was celebrating hard tonight.

Things have been going pretty well with Brittany, but I was feeling like something was missing. The communication was still off. I didn't know if I was pleasing her, because she never let me know what she wanted. It felt like she didn't care either way.

She now answered the phone most of the time I called, and whenever I wanted to see her, I let her know in advance, so that was cool. But, I still felt like I needed to step it up a notch. We went to the same college, but I would never see her during the day due to different class schedules. I'd see all these other couples around campus holding hands, kissing, and walking each other to class, and I kind of wanted that for us.

So, I was at her house this morning so that I could drive

her to campus. I figured I could walk her to her first class at least, like so many couples did in the movies. Brittany was a gem, and all I wanted to do was show her off.

I didn't even get to ring the doorbell, because she came flying out of the house just as I was about to. What surprised me was that there was a guy behind her. He looked familiar, like I'd seen him on campus or something, but I had no idea who he was. I wondered if he were her brother or cousin.

"Hey Dedrick. What are you doing here? Didn't I tell you not to come by unannounced?"

"I just...I thought...I wanted to drive you to school today." I stuck my hand out to walk her to my car, but the dude behind her smacked it.

"Take yo' ass back wherever the fuck you came from, bruh. She's good."

Brittany turned around to face him. Shaking her head, she whined, "Stop, Julius." Then, she looked at me. "Look, Dedrick. I think you're really nice, but...I told you the other day, I don't know what you want from me. This right here... this probably won't be much between us. You're not my type."

How could she say that? After all the times we'd made love, and after I told her I wanted to treat her like a princess, she still doubted me? That wasn't fair.

"Please. Go. And don't come back." Brittany walked past me, holding the hand of the rude guy, and they got in the car that was parked on the side of her house.

Watching the two of them leave together tore me up

inside. I had a surprise for her, too. Reaching into my pocket, I opened the box holding the promise ring I'd planned to give her, and quickly closed it shut before I cried.

L *ater that day...*

"That's exactly why before Bailee, I wasn't taking these bitches serious, bruh. I told you Brittany was a hoe. You should've left that bitch alone after you hit the first time. You used a condom, right?" Domino lifted his eyebrow and took a swig of his beer.

After my class was over, I'd come to The Black Palace to talk to him about what happened this morning with Brittany. I felt so betrayed and angry; the one girl I wanted more than life itself had hurt me and didn't seem to have any remorse about doing so.

I thought about ignoring Domino's question, but I answered truthfully. "No, I didn't." Common sense would've told anybody to, but when it came to Brittany, I didn't use common sense. She was so perfect to me, and I wanted to experience all of her; I didn't want anything rubber in my way.

"You heard me, nigga?" Domino interrupted my thoughts. I hadn't heard anything he said, because my mind was consumed with thoughts of Brittany. "You need to go get tested. Your dick is probably gon' burn off."

"What do you mean? I'm burning when I pee, but I figured that was normal after having sex, since it's now been exposed to other skin."

"You've been exposed, alright. The only time your shit is gon' burn is if you fucked a hoe. Take yo' stupid ass to the doctor, man. That bitch probably gave you an STD."

Good grief. Today couldn't get any better, could it?

A few days later...

I found out that Brittany had indeed given me gonorrhea. It would be just my luck that the very first sexual partner I had, gave me a disease. The good thing was that it was curable, but I was angry as hell for not believing my older brother when he warned me about these females. Never again would I put my trust in a girl. I gave her all my attention, all my time, and my virginity, just for her to turn around and play me. I felt like the dummy that my brother and his friends were insinuating that I was.

"That's why you don't trust these hoes," Terrell laughed, as he smacked one of the strippers' butts as she danced in front of him.

We were at The Black Palace, which was bittersweet for me, because although I was having a good time, I was reminded of Brittany when I came here. This was where we formally met, and now I couldn't stop thinking about her infidelity. Did monogamy mean nothing, anymore?

"Not all women are bad, man. Hoes. Those are the ones you dick down and keep it moving. A good woman, like my girl, you lock down." Domino chimed in, puffing on his cigar.

"I know now."

Domino snapped his fingers, in order to get one of the strippers' attention. "My brother's going through some shit, ma. Give that nigga a dance."

The stripper was so pretty and thick, with a huge round ass that she sat directly on my lap as she clapped her cheeks together to the rhythm of the song. Just as she was finishing up her dance, Domino tapped me on the shoulder.

"Your shorty's coming."

I turned around to see Brittany, charging toward the VIP area. She had a black eye and a busted lip, but was rolling up in here like she wanted to fight. Looks like she'd already been in one, and lost. "Dedrick! I need to talk to you!"

"We don't have shit to talk about, bitch! So take your motherfucking bitch hoe ass out of here! Shit, shit, shit!" I yelled, surprising everyone, including myself, with my harsh tone. I guess being around Domino and his friends had rubbed off on me, because I no longer had sympathy for her. She'd taken advantage of my kindness and now, I was ready to show her just what she was missing.

"Dedrick! Please let me talk to you!" Brittany whined, trying to get through the partition. Vince stopped her, though.

"Bitch, go talk to the next nigga! You ain't giving out anything but STDs and headaches; fuck you!"

"Oh shit!" Terrell and Domino erupted in laughter, dapping me up.

I made eye contact with Vince and requested that he put

her out of the club, which he did. She was yelling my name and crying as she was being escorted out, but oh well; she should've wanted me when I wanted her. I hate to say it, but she'd ruined it for the next girl, because my heart was now ice cold. Who could blame me, though?

Chapter Twenty-Two

BAILEE RODGERS

A few days later...

oday was the day! My parents and Domino were finally going to meet later on this evening, and although I was a nervous wreck, I was finally ready. I knew I couldn't keep hiding him forever, and I was finally at a point where I didn't care what people thought about our relationship. I think that was the best thing – I loved him, he loved me, and nobody could take that away from us. Dom wasn't a bad guy either – he was just crazy as hell. Well, he met his match in me, because I constantly proved to him I wasn't one of those weak bitches he used to. And because unlike every other female who'd ever been in life, I set standards, he respected me. He had no choice.

Stepping out of the shower, looking like a chocolate God, Domino scooped me in his arms and smothered me with kisses. "You know I love you right?" I loved how affectionate he was. There wasn't a day that went by where I didn't get a kiss that made my toes curl or an orgasm that took my breath away.

"You better. You don't have a choice."

Mounting me on top of him, Domino laid me down on our bed and dove into my lady garden with his wet tongue. Thank God I was no longer bleeding, because this was one of my favorite things to get from him...

"Umm. Damn Bai. Your shit tastes good. Like pineapples and shit."

If I were able to talk, I would've thanked him, but since he'd sucked the orgasm out of me, all I could do was moan and enjoy the way his tongue felt brushing against my clit, over and over again...

A few days later... Everything went well a few days ago, when my parents met Domino. Which was a surprise to me, because usually my mom could be a complete bitch; she wasn't that day, though. I found out from Dom after we left their house that he knew my dad from being a frequent at The Gentleman's Corner, which was funny because I'd never known my dad to visit strip clubs.

I was just glad the whole meet and greet ordeal was over. They liked him, he liked them, and now we could move on. I was finally at a point in my life where I felt that I was at peace. My friendships, my relationship, my family life, and professional life were all...peaceful. There was no drama and no dishonesty coming from any party I dealt with. I was even starting to get over the abortion I had, because in my heart, I knew I'd give Domino a child when the timing was right. What more could I ask for?

With the opening night of The Black Palace Miami now being one week away, my man was running around like a chicken with his head cut off, trying to make sure everything was perfect. Domino wouldn't admit it, but I think he was nervous about how well the new location did because it would determine whether other locations he was looking at would be successful.

Him and Weezy and were actually back in Miami now; they left this morning and would be back tomorrow. So, I was playing Domino for the day at The Black Palace location here in Columbia. I only had class on Tuesdays and Thursdays, so since today was Friday, I was free and able to hold down for the fort here for my man. That is, if Tatianna would get out of my way and let me. I understood that she was the manager he'd hired, but I was his woman, and my position was above hers any day of the week.

"Is there something you're looking for in particular, Bailee?" Tatianna asked, watching me from the hallway. I was moving things around in Dom's office, simply because it was a little cluttered, and I was the one of us with slight OCD.

Tatianna was staring at me like she wanted to start something, and she had the right one tonight.

The bitch was already treading on very thin ice with me, because of that shit she tried with my man in Miami. She didn't know that I knew, because I told Domino I was willing to forgive and forget; but I never promised I wouldn't beat her ass *again*.

Closing the drawer shut, I smirked shook my head slowly. "I don't think you understand my position, Tatianna. I'm his girlfriend. I don't need a reason to be in here. And since he left me in charge, I'd say you're out of line for even asking me that question. You can go man the front; I'll handle back here."

Tatianna slammed the door to Domino's office behind her as she walked in. "I might've let you slide for putting your hands on me once before, Bailee, but that'll never happen again. As a matter of fact, if you don't do this favor for me, I'll tell Domino your little secret."

"What secret?"

Smirking, Tatianna whipped out her cell phone from her bra and held up several pictures of me leaving the abortion clinic. Sneaky bitch.

"How did you get that?" My heart raced as thoughts of Domino finding out I'd aborted a child that was possibly his crossed my mind. We'd talked about kids a few times, and he made it clear that he wanted them with me. He probably would never forgive me if he found out. "What favor do you need, Tatianna?" As much as I hated this bitch, I was desperate. I worked too hard to build this relationship with Dom to let this hoe tear it down.

"I'm glad you asked. I've been trying to get him to do business with a gentleman by the name of James Montclair. He's not feeling it. I need you to make him agree, or he'll just happen to see pictures of your little trip. How does that sound?"

"It sounds like I should've fucked you up when I had the chance. Get out of this office, Tatianna."

She winked her eye at me and then walked out, leaving me to wallow in my misery. Just when I thought things were going well, there was always some bullshit that got in the way. It felt like I just couldn't catch a break.

*O*pening night of *The Black Palace Miami…*
Staring at Domino's fine ass as he got the club hyped made me smile uncontrollably while my pussy throbbed continuously. He was so damn sexy, and not only that, but his ambition was unmatched. My man was so excited about tonight, and I was proud as fuck of him for this moment. It was crazy to think that I'd met him on the opening night of his Columbia location, and now, only three months later, we were together and in love, with a second location in Miami. The Black Palace Miami was lit as hell; I'm sure the King of Diamonds wasn't making any money tonight. The crowd in here was so thick, you could hardly move, and the line was still out the door with people wanting to get in.

The cages were the main attraction, and all the girls we'd chosen to work here looked sexy as hell climbing out of them, then swinging down the poles. The VIP area in this building was bigger than in the Columbia location, so it was a little more room to move around. Me, Janay, and Camiyah danced our asses off for our men while the strippers entertained everyone else.

This was my first time meeting Camiyah, and from what I could tell, she was cool as fuck. She seemed to be a good mom, even though I had no idea where her baby was since we were in Miami, and she seemed to really care about Davion, even though at times I wondered if she were just a tad bit afraid of him. That's the thing about heavy drug users, though – one minute they were calm, and the next, they were trying to attack you. Celine told me about what went down in the library between them, and although I didn't approve of the way he'd come at her, I was glad she'd come out unscathed. Had he hurt her, we would've had some serious issues.

I didn't even think he'd be coming, since he and Dom fell out, but that just shows you how soft my man was on his baby brother. So, I had no choice but to accept him. Even though I couldn't stand his ass, I felt like he needed someone like Camiyah in his corner, because she seemed to calm him down. We all flew down together yesterday, and I could count on one hand how many disrespectful things he'd said so far. And for him, that was miraculous. I just hoped he kept up his good behavior, because I didn't want nothing or nobody to ruin my baby's special night or weekend.

A part of me wished Celine could've come with her new boo Eric, but Davion would've had a fit, and Celine wouldn't have been comfortable either. So, she was missing all the fun here, but it wasn't like she was lonely.

The six of us partied our asses off, and although the club was supposed to close at four, people didn't start leaving until after five. Dom wanted to stay until everyone left, so we didn't leave the building until after six. My feet, which were in a new pair of Giuseppe heels my man had bought for me for this special occasion, were hurting like a motherfucker. I was ready to get to the hotel, let Dom run me a bath, and lay in his arms for hours.

We loaded into the Escalade that Domino had rented for this trip, and by the time I opened my eyes again, we were pulling up at the hotel. I hugged Janay and Camiyah, and all the couples went into our respective rooms. Domino had sex on his mind, while all I wanted to do was sleep. But, because I was so proud of all my man had accomplished, I had no issue with giving him some good dome and pussy. After all, he deserved it.

By the time we finished both rounds, it was well after eight. He had worn me out with that monster between his legs, but I wasn't complaining.

"Let's shower." Dom pulled me from the bed and led me to the spacious bathroom, where he washed my body and then served me with head before we got out. He always knew just how I liked it...

I got cozy in the bed, and Dom decided to go get some ice

from down the hall. Right after he walked out the room, there was a knock on the door, and when I went to open it, I couldn't believe who had the audacity to be standing there. I wanted to slap the smile from across the face of......

To be continued...